Paige

SPRINGSONG ❧ BOOKS

Andrea

Anne

Carrie

Colleen

Cynthia

Gillian

Jenny

Joanna

Kara

Kathy

Leslie

Lisa

Melissa

Michelle

Paige

Sara

Sherri

Tiffany

Paige

Judy Baer

BETHANY HOUSE PUBLISHERS
MINNEAPOLIS, MINNESOTA 55438

Paige
Judy Baer

Library of Congress Catalog Card Number 86–70912

All scripture quotations, unless indicated, are taken from
the Revised Standard Version of the Bible, copyrighted
1946, 1952, 1971 by the Division of Christian Education
of the National Council of Churches of Christ in the
USA. Used by permission.

ISBN 1–55661–585–X

Published by Bethany House Publishers
A Ministry of Bethany Fellowship, Inc.
11300 Hampshire Avenue South
Minneapolis, Minnesota 55438

Printed in the United States of America

For Adrian C. Fox—
Thanks for your enthusiasm.

JUDY BAER received a B.A. in English and Education from Concordia College in Moorhead, Minnesota. She has had over thirty novels published and is a member of the National Romance Writers of America, the Society of Children's Book Writers, and the National Federation of Press Women.

Two of her novels, *Adrienne* and *Paige*, have been prize-winning bestsellers in the Bethany House SPRING-FLOWER SERIES (for girls 12–15). Both books have been awarded first place for juvenile fiction in the National Federation of Press Women's communications contest.

1

*T*he stranger was back.

What's more, Paige Bradshaw's parents were behaving mysteriously. She could see it in their eyes, in their actions. Apprehension. Fear. And something more. What, Paige did not understand.

She'd been too young to notice something as intangible as fear the first time the stranger had appeared at their farm door though instinctively she'd known her parents were upset. The only time she'd seen them more so was the day Grandmother died. And what a black time that had been.

Paige would always connect her grandmother's death with the stranger's first appearance. The tall, shadowy man had arrived only hours after the sad yet joyous funeral service at their little country church. Grandmother was safe and happy with her Lord. Paige and her parents were left to mourn the empty spot at the dinner table and miss the gentle swishing of her rocker as she crocheted myriad doilies.

The stranger's visit had somehow heightened her parents' grief. But they had kept the reasons from Paige, carrying on whispered conversations that lasted long into the night. That was most alarming of all to the fourteen-year-old whose family had never before kept secrets.

Now he was back, and her parents were acting *that way* again. Nervous. Afraid. But Paige was one year older, ten years wiser, and a hundred percent more curious. This time she would not let her parents placate her with meaningless phrases. She would learn who the stranger was—whether her parents wanted her to or not.

"Mom?" Paige dangled a lazy finger over the steam rising from the pot her mother had just carried to the table. Her brown hair shone in the sunlight streaming through the kitchen window.

"Hmmm? Don't burn yourself, dear. This is very hot." Ellen Bradshaw patted the sides of the cast iron kettle with mitted hands. "I think this jelly is going to be very nice. All those plums you and your dad picked will pay off." Methodically, she straightened a row of glasses of all shapes and sizes and began to spoon shimmering pink liquid into the nearest jar.

"Who is he, Mom? The man who was here last night?" Paige watched her mother carefully as she posed the question. Her dark eyes followed her mother's precise movements.

Her parents had tried to act like the tall, sad-faced man had not stood on their front porch last evening. They didn't know Paige had seen him from her perch on the picnic table where she sat sorting plums. She'd seen him grip his felt hat with nervous fingers and heard him speak in low, subversive tones. *If only she'd heard what he said!*

Ellen's steady hand began to quiver. The crystal liquid danced in the ladle like a pink wave at high tide.

"It's none of your business, Paige. It was something to do with your father, not you." Her tone was sharp.

A year ago that would have been enough to silence her questions. But Paige was only a month away from sixteen now. Whatever it was that disturbed her mother and father so deeply *was* her business too.

"But it is, Mom! Daddy barked at me this morning for

no reason at all. Then he fell all over himself apologizing. You two whispered half the night—"

"It has nothing to do with you, Paige."

"—and I heard you crying."

Ellen let the big-bowled spoon clatter into the pot. Then, with as little care, she slumped into the ladder-backed chair across from Paige. Reaching across the oil-cloth, she entwined her fingers with her daughter's.

"Please, honey, let it drop. The man who came last night upset your father and me. He's a charlatan, making some outrageous claims. Your dad will take care of it. Trust him."

"What kind of claims?" Paige persisted. Her mother's response had only increased her curiosity. She had not spent every summer of her childhood reading mysteries for nothing. "About the farm?"

"You might say so. And," Ellen stood resolutely, "I'm not going to say any more. If your father chooses to discuss it with you, then I will too. But, believe me, Paige, it's nothing to do with you."

"Yes it is!" Paige murmured, but Ellen had already made her way into the pantry. Somehow, that dark-suited man had turned her peaceful family life upside down. Her normally placid father was scolding her for no reason; her mother was on the brink of tears. Even the puppy barked nervously when the man came around.

A low whine and a cold, wet nose broke into her musings. Bonzo tugged at her shirt-sleeve. The stranger's visit had not changed everything. The puppy still wanted to play.

"Come on, fellow," Paige acquiesced. "You win. Where's your ball?" The pair made their way through the screen door and onto the gravel driveway that circled in front of the big old farmhouse.

Bonzo skidded to a halt near his red rubber ball, nicked and scarred from hours of vigorous chewing. Mauling the ball with his paws, he pounced and played with it until Paige picked it up and tossed it toward the lightpole in the middle of the yard.

As Bonzo romped and tumbled toward the red missile, Paige's eyes scanned the familiar scene. The farm buildings were built in a circle, their fronts facing inward, like the prairie schooners in a wagon train, circling together to protect themselves from outside intrusion.

House. Woodshed. Bunkhouse. Garage. Chicken house. Barn. Paige ticked off each building on a mental checklist. There'd been nothing new built here in her lifetime, and little in her father's. Grandfather had constructed it all in the years after he came to settle in North Dakota.

The red buildings sparkled in the morning sun. Paige and her father had spent two weeks painting the buildings "barn red." Every barn within miles sported the same bright crimson.

But otherwise it was an uncommon morning. The farmyard crackled with invisible energy. The sun seemed more intense, the grass greener, the sky bluer, and the air more crisp and invigorating. Even her father's slow, deliberate movements seemed quicker as he hurried toward her. His distinctive rambling gait slowed as he neared.

"Hi, Daddy."

"Hello, Chapter. What are you up to?"

Paige winced, then smiled. At least her father had returned to normal. When she was tiny—and a rather undisciplined handful, to hear her mother tell it—he'd always commented she was more work than a Paige, that they should have named her Chapter instead and the name had stuck. She gave a gusty sigh of relief. The tension she'd felt last night dissipated.

"Bonzo was begging to play. My chores are done."

"You're starting the summer on the right foot, Paige. I

like to see you get at your work early. Then you can have the afternoons to yourself."

"If Evan doesn't come wandering over to drive me crazy," she grumbled. Evan and his sullen ways could ruin a day faster than anything.

"Don't talk about your cousin like that, Paige. He's a nice enough boy. Give him a chance."

"I've given him a dozen chances, Daddy. No matter how nice I am to him, he expects more. He's either clinging to me like glue or stomping off because he thinks I've done something to insult him. No matter what I do, Evan doesn't seem to like it."

"Patience, Paige. Patience. Evan's a very insecure boy. You've got to give him time."

"Sometimes I wonder why Aunt Lois bothered to adopt him. A baby would have been a lot easier."

"But there are lots of people willing to adopt babies. Not so many want to take on a ten-year-old boy."

"Well, he's fifteen now, shouldn't he be improving soon?" Paige wrinkled her nose in irritation, knowing full-well she'd make the effort to be nice to Evan for her aunt's sake. Maybe Evan was her cross to bear. She'd read about that in Scripture somewhere. Perhaps that would give her the patience she needed to deal with her cousin.

Mike Bradshaw chuckled. "The boy needs love and acceptance, Paige. You've just forgotten how frightened and alone he was when he came to live with Lois. He *has* improved, you know."

"Well, I suppose he couldn't help it. Anybody would improve just living with Aunt Lois," she grudgingly admitted. There wasn't a sunnier, sweeter woman alive. Aunt Lois had introduced her whole family to Jesus. If she couldn't help mold Evan through persistence and prayer, no one could.

"Keep that in mind when the going gets rough between

you and your cousin," Mike Bradshaw advised. "When things get out of hand, do like my sister does. Take it to the Lord. He'll give you patience." Mike laid a fatherly arm across Paige's shoulders. He smelled like grass and fuel oil and warm skin. Farm smells. Paige closed her eyes and inhaled deeply. She loved living on a farm.

Before she could open them again, the friendly arm stiffened around her. She felt her father's sharp intake of breath. The relaxed fingers that draped over her upper arm suddenly tightened.

Her eyes flew open in surprise. Her father was always so gentle. The sting of his tightening grip shocked Paige more than hurt her.

Immediately she saw what had caused her father's reaction. The man was back. He'd coasted his vintage Chevrolet into the yard, the motor silent. Bonzo had heard as little of his approach as she. Now he started to bark with the insulted yelps of a foiled guard dog.

"Stop it!" Mike Bradshaw's voice cut through the racket.

Bonzo was immediately contrite and plopped backward onto his hind legs. Though he quivered with intense excitement, he stayed silent. Paige scratched the pup comfortingly as her father strode toward the visitor.

When Bonzo calmed down, Paige stood up and began to stroll toward the two men. Unless her father sent her to the house, she was going to listen to their conversation.

Somehow she sensed that what the stranger had to say was going to affect her profoundly. Suddenly the mystery she'd vowed to solve seemed far less exciting, but the lurking question remained.

What *did* this man want from her family? And why?

He was taller than her father by several inches. His height and the dark coat he wore made him loom over Mike Bradshaw like some sort of phantom. Paige shook herself.

Her imagination was getting out of hand. Next she'd be seeing him as the boogeyman!

He was a perfectly nice-looking man, she assured herself. Dark-haired and pale, not unlike her father. As he stood waiting for Mike Bradshaw to speak, Paige took a quick assessment of the man's features. The corner of her lip quirked in amusement. He reminded her of a beagle— sorrowful, droopy eyes, folds of extra skin in the deep creases at the corners of his lips, and a brow so furrowed it looked as though some farmer had just come through it with a plow.

The man looked so sad! Even the defeated hunch of his shoulders spoke of sadness. Paige's footsteps quickened. She wanted to hear what he was going to say.

"Mr. Bradshaw," the man began. His voice was low, like the distant rumble of a freight train.

"What are you doing here, Gardner? I've told you before that you aren't welcome on this farm." Her father's voice was sharp and cold as steel.

"I realize that, but I had to come back. I had to know if either you or your wife had reconsidered, if either of you would agree to look for the information I'm seeking. If you'd just examine the family Bible, or whatever old records . . ." His voice held a note of desperation.

"Sir, you've disrupted my family enough. I've lived on this farm all my life. My wife came here as a bride nearly twenty years ago. If we *were* going to find this . . ." Bradshaw broke off as he realized that Paige was standing behind him. As Mike turned to address her, Gardner's eyes followed him.

"Paige, I want you to take Bonzo and go to the barn."

"Daddy," she began, but was stopped by the fierce scowl her father gave her.

"Now. I don't want to discuss it."

"Yessir," she mumbled with disappointment. She'd

never find out what the stranger wanted if she were sent to the barn every time a clue-gathering opportunity arose.

She turned around and scuffled her toes in the gravel, kicking and spraying little gray pebbles as she walked. Nancy Drew or the fantastic Hercule Poirot of the novels she loved to read would never tolerate such an interruption to *their* sleuthing. Then again, Mike Bradshaw wasn't their father, either.

Walking as slowly as she could to still be considered moving, Paige heard the last fragments of the conversation between the two men.

"It's got to be here! There's got to be something that proves—"

"There is nothing on this farm that concerns you, Mr. Gardner. Absolutely nothing. I only ask that you leave and not bother my family again."

Paige reached the barn and turned back to watch the two men. Bradshaw had the older man by the elbow and was steering him toward the car.

Squinting into the sun, Paige blurred the two forms into a hazy outline as they walked toward the battered Chevy. Her eyes flew open in surprise. The puzzling Mr. Gardner and her father were difficult to tell apart from a distance. Only Gardner's extra height made them distinguishable from across the farmyard.

Paige shrugged. It was their shoulders that made them look alike. Her father's had grown round with worry since Grandma died. The heavy stoop of the men's shoulders made them mirror images.

"I have no knowledge of what you're asking! None at all! Now get off my land!" Bradshaw's voice carried on a gust of wind to Paige in the barn's arch. Her eyes were round and worried as she turned to the dusky interior of the barn.

Paige had never heard her father raise his voice in anger. It wasn't right, he said. Whatever drove him to it must be very serious indeed.

The odors and dimness of the barn welcomed her. She loved the barn. It was shady and cool today. Most of the cattle were in the pasture. Only two milk cows were dipping their heads into the feeders that ran the center length of the building.

Paige sauntered up to a tan and white Guernsey and crooned in her ear, "Hello, Bossy, how are you today?" The cow turned liquid brown eyes on Paige, as if to say, "Fine, thanks. How are you?"

The milk cow ground unceasingly at her cud. A stalk of hay angled out of her mouth. Paige laid her head next to the cow's ear. She could smell fresh sweet grass and the powdery smell of feed. "Nice Bossy. Nice Bossy."

Paige glanced around. The raw wood walls were dark with age. Sunlight streaming through the windows caught motes of dust and made a whirling dance in the river of light shining on the planked floor.

The clip-clop of hooved feet made her glance up. Lady Blue, a trim Arabian mare, stood curiously in the far door of the barn. The pony pawed daintily with one hoof and then pranced sideways away from the door.

"Oh, no you don't, Lady Blue!" Paige laughed. "Don't beg for a ride until I find out what's going on up at the house!" The horse bobbed its head. The skin along its back flickered and shimmied as a horsefly landed on its spine. Paige pointed a finger in her mare's direction. "Stay there. I'm going up to the house to ask Daddy what's going on. Then we'll go for a ride."

The old Chevy was missing from the roadway as Paige neared the farmhouse. The mysterious Mr. Gardner was gone.

Paige's jaw jutted out in determination as she walked. This time she wouldn't let her parents sidestep her questions. This time, she would get the answers she sought. She had every right to know who this Mr. Gardner was and what he wanted. Every right. . . .

The storybook sleuths with whom she whiled away so many of her leisure hours marched in her head in a motley parade. Sherlock Holmes. Nancy Drew. The Hardy Boys. Trixie Belden. Christie's Poirot and Marple. Master detectives, all of them. And Paige Bradshaw too. She would find out why the stranger's visits inspired such turmoil—why her father's shoulders stooped even further—why her mother cried.

She felt a nudge of adrenalin pump through her veins. This little mystery was exciting, far better than reading about it in a musty old book. Here was a real live mystery to solve. Perhaps this was something to help alleviate the long, boring summer that was looming on the horizon.

"Mom? Dad? Are you in here?"

The house was still. Paige walked the circle of rooms that led her back to the door at which she had entered. Silence. Then a voice drifted down from the second floor.

"I just don't understand it, Mike! If something like that had happened, wouldn't your mother have . . ." Paige tiptoed to the foot of the stairs.

"You know how my mother was, Ellen. There wasn't a more closed-mouthed woman in three counties. If she'd had a secret she wanted to keep . . ."

"But *that* kind of a secret? I can't imagine anyone being able to . . ."

" 'The tongue is a fire . . . no human being can tame the tongue—a restless evil, full of poison.' Can't you just hear Ma saying that?"

"I suppose you're right, but I . . ." Suddenly Paige realized what she was doing. Eavesdropping. Guiltily, she made some noise on the step. No matter how curious she was, she had no business listening in on other people's private conversations. That was tantamount to stealing.

"Mom? Dad?"

Her parents dashed from their bedroom to meet her at the top of the stairs. Her mother had been crying again. Her father's hair was rumpled, as though he'd been running agitated fingers through the dark curls.

"Are you guys all right?" Paige blurted.

"Fine. Just fine. I thought you were in the barn."

"I came in to . . ." she bit her lip before she nearly said, "ask you about the stranger." It didn't seem the time to upset them further. "To ask if I could take Lady Blue out for a ride."

"I think that would be a good idea, honey." Ellen Bradshaw was an older reflection of Paige—brunet and brown-eyed with ivory skin and a natural, polished luster to her cheeks. But today she seemed tired, tired and afraid.

Paige suppressed the thought. Her parents were never afraid. Her enthusiasm for the mystery ebbed a bit as she studied the pair at the top of the stairs. Then her buoyant, inquisitive nature returned.

"Beth said they got a big batch of new kittens. Eleven of them."

"You'd better go and check that out," Mr. Bradshaw smiled. "Eleven sounds like a record-breaking litter to me."

Paige nodded her head. She needed to think. A ride on Lady Blue and a visit at the York's might help. Beth and her older brother Bryan always made her feel better.

When she returned to the barn, Lady Blue was dancing restlessly at the gate. Paige flung a blanket over her back and tossed a light saddle across the wide expanse of the horse's mid-section. Lady Blue nuzzled at Paige's pocket while the girl tightened the cinch.

"No sugar cubes today, Kiddo. You're on a diet."

Lady Blue gave her an extra hard nudge.

"No matter how hard you beg, Lady. Only apples for

you from now on—and we're out of them today."

Lady Blue pawed the ground in complaint.

As Paige swung into the saddle, Lady Blue quit begging and broke into a trot.

Paige threw her head back and savored the feel of warm wind licking at her neck. It was going to be an unusual summer, she realized. She could sense it already. The stranger. Her parents' odd behavior. Her own curiosity. A mystery to solve.

Paige made a vow as she rode. By fall, when the leaves began to turn and the school bus rolled into the yard, she would have solved the mystery that was unfolding before her. She'd get to the heart of the problem. There was nothing that Paige liked better than a puzzle.

Nothing, that is, except the thought that Bryan York might begin to realize that his little neighbor Paige Bradshaw was growing up.

2

*P*aige hoisted herself to a standing position in the saddle, her feet wedged tight against the stirrups. She scanned the landscape. The North Dakota flatness was really a series of gently undulating hills, too shallow for the eye to register from a distance but steep enough to vary the contour of the land. Greens of every hue met her eye. The black earth was springing to life with fresh blades of grain marching in endless rows. The trees were heavy with new greenery, the air fresh, the sun bright.

She gave Lady Blue a nudge with the heels of her riding boots. "Come on, Lady, let's go see Beth."

Beth was sitting glumly on the front porch of her rambling old farmhouse picking eyes from potatoes in a burlap sack. Blackie, her pup and brother to Bonzo, sat at her feet. Beth brightened considerably when Paige galloped into the yard.

"Hi! I'm so glad you're here!"

Paige swung off Lady Blue. "Did you miss me? School's only been out two days."

"Not exactly. Mom told me if I couldn't find anything else to do I should pick these potatoes." She wrinkled her nose. "They smell like mold and old dirt. Now that you're here I don't have to do this."

"You sure know how to make a girl feel welcome," Paige commented dryly.

Beth wrinkled her freckled nose again. Paige studied

her friend. Beth was tiny, red-haired, and perpetually scat-terbrained. Her mouth was usually in gear before her brain. She shrugged and smiled brightly. "You're used to me, Paige. You know I didn't mean it. Bryan says I'm lucky I've got you for a friend 'cause everyone else would've run off when I opened my mouth."

Paige grinned. Bryan was right. Beth took some getting used to. Then Paige felt another smile building inside. Bryan. He'd said something nice about her. That was def-initely worth smiling about.

Beth was chattering like a magpie as Paige pulled her thoughts away from Bryan York.

". . . don't you? I mean, really, three months of chores! The only person in the whole world who likes chores is my brother Bryan. I think summers get so *boring*. I mean . . ."

"You're rattling like a rock in a tin can, Beth." Bryan came up behind the two girls, wiping his grease-stained hands on his even more grease-stained jeans.

"Oh! You startled me! Don't scare me like that!" Beth scolded him like a little wet hen.

Paige and Bryan burst into laughter.

"Beth, you're scared of your own shadow," Paige re-minded her.

Beth had the grace to look chagrined. "Just because I don't like those dumb mystery stories you two read doesn't mean I'm not brave! I could solve a mystery if I had to!" She grinned and her eyes sparkled with mischief, "But I'm glad there aren't a lot of mysteries around here—other than what's for supper tonight!"

Paige chewed thoughtfully on the corner of her lip. There were more mysteries around than Beth knew. Her mother and father and the stranger came to mind. That was a mystery if anything was. Before she could decide whether or not to mention the situation, Bryan spoke.

"I'd better get back to work. Dad wants this tractor running by suppertime."

Paige watched him walk toward the John Deere and hunker down beside the big green tractor.

Bryan was only two years older than she and Beth, but he seemed so much more mature. Farm boys were that way, she decided. Early responsibility made them seem older and wiser. It didn't hurt that he was handsome, either. While Beth's hair was the color of flames, Bryan's was a rich burnished copper. He had none of Beth's freckles and none of her flightiness.

Paige sighed. She wished Bryan would discover that she was more than Beth's best friend. She was tired of being treated like his second little sister. For once she'd like being treated like . . . well, like . . . his girlfriend!

"Whatcha thinking about?"

Paige felt her cheeks burning. Beth looked at her curiously as she blushed. Caught thinking about Bryan! How embarrassing.

"Oh, nothing much," Paige stammered. "Didn't you say you had some new kittens?"

"Sure." Beth gave her friend a sideways glance. "Come on."

Beth was quiet all the way to the barn. Paige could almost see the wheels turning in her inquisitive little mind. She'd have to be more careful from now on.

If Beth got the idea that her friend had a crush on her big brother, she'd dash to Bryan with the news. Anyway, Paige thought to herself, she couldn't date until her sixteenth birthday and that was still a month away. No use thinking about things she couldn't do anything about.

The kittens mewed and tumbled about in a nest of straw. The mother cat had tried to hide them, but eleven babies had overwhelmed her a bit and she'd finally settled on giving birth in an empty cardboard box in the loft.

"Aren't they tiny?" Paige breathed. The little gray and black balls of fur were like a miracle. Their eyes weren't open yet. Instinctively they nestled near the mother cat who eyed the two girls suspiciously.

"I don't think MomCat wants us here," Beth commented.

"MomCat?"

"Yup. MomCat and TomCat. Mother and dad to this brood. Do you want a kitten when they get older?"

"Maybe. If my folks say it's okay. And if Bonzo agrees." Paige stared off at the pigeons roosting along a rope strung from the hayloft doors. Their gentle coo lulled her restless mind. Absently she stroked MomCat.

"Beth?"

"Hmmm?" Beth's nose was buried in a kitten's fur.

"Do your parents sometimes keep . . . secrets . . . from you?"

"Sure. All the time."

"They do?" Paige eyed her friend in surprise.

"Sure. Christmas presents. Birthdays. . . ."

"No, I mean *real* secrets."

"Those too. Mom and Dad didn't tell me Aunt Katie was going to have a baby until . . ."

"Not like that!"

"Well, what then?" Beth sounded disgusted. "I don't understand."

"I guess I don't either," Paige admitted. She put the kitten she'd picked up next to its mother. The older cat visibly relaxed to have her brood intact again.

"I think you'd better explain." Beth rocked back on her haunches, looking like a red-haired pixie perched in the straw.

Paige smiled. "I can't. I don't know what I'm talking about."

Beth shrugged cheerfully. "Why should that stop you? It never stops me!"

The girls' laughter echoed in the vast hay mow. Paige stretched her long legs and stood. She ran frustrated fingers through the tumble of long brown hair and brushed away the straw clinging to her jeans. "Forget it, Beth."

Beth nodded amiably. "For now. Let's go make some brownies. I always think better when I'm eating. And anyway"—glancing slyly at Paige and looking as though she knew more than she let on—"Bryan *loves* brownies."

The York kitchen was heavy with the fragrance of chocolate when Bryan sauntered through nearly an hour later.

"Smells good in here."

"Tastes even better." Paige handed him a plate of fresh bars.

"Looks good! Thanks. So what are your plans for the summer, Paige?" Bryan inquired as he poured himself a glass of milk from the refrigerator.

She sat down on the padded bench that angled in one corner of the kitchen. Curling her legs beneath her, she shrugged. "I'm not sure. Helping out around the farm, I suppose. Teaching Bonzo some tricks. Cooking, ironing, mowing grass . . ."

"Nothing fun?"

She smiled. "Reading. I've already sent to the state library for—"

"You mean you've already exhausted the supply of 'whodunnits' in our library?"

"Leave her alone, Beth. Just because the cover of a Sherlock Holmes mystery scares you doesn't mean Paige can't like them."

"You guys are weird," Beth remarked. "What's so fun about reading 'The Case of the Missing Crowbar'?"

"You'll never understand, Beth. You just don't have any sense of adventure," Bryan assured his sister.

"Adventure? Who needs it? I get all the chills and thrills I need in algebra class. I'm just thankful summer's here and I don't have to do quadratic equations any longer."

Bryan and Paige grinned at each other behind Beth's back. You were either a mystery buff or you weren't. Beth was obviously in the second category.

For a moment Paige was tempted to mention the personal mystery that seemed to be unfolding at her home. She was sure Bryan would keep the information to himself, but Beth—dear, blabber-mouth Beth—would probably be sounding it from the rooftop before dusk.

Paige wiped away an imaginary crumb on the leg of her jeans. "Well, gotta be going."

"So soon?" Beth sounded disappointed.

"Already?" Was that disappointment in Bryan's voice too?

"Yeh. Mom likes help with supper."

"When will you be back?"

Paige's head jerked upward as though it were attached to marionette strings. Bryan was wondering when she'd be back!

"I'm not sure. I'd like to come over tomorrow, but I think Evan is going to be around the farm all day. He's supposed to help me plant the garden."

"You have to spend the day with Evan?" Beth grimaced. "What a way to start the summer vacation!"

"That's not nice, Beth," Bryan chided.

"It's okay," Paige defended her friend. "I know that Evan is pretty difficult to like, but he's getting better. He just takes some getting used to."

"Why'd your aunt adopt him in the first place, Paige? Why would a single lady like Lois Bradshaw want a son, anyway? He's always so . . . snide. Everything he says sounds so mean." Beth's pert little face crumpled a bit.

"Every time he talks to me he hurts my feelings. I'm kinda, I dunno, scared of him."

"Evan is insecure. That's what my dad says. He says we'd be insecure too if we'd been moved from foster home to foster home for the first ten years of our lives. Dad says Evan uses that nasty tough-guy routine for protection. When he's sure our family has accepted him and loves him, then he'll lose that attitude."

"Seems like he'd be pretty tough to love," Beth concluded. "I'd have a hard time."

Sometimes Paige found it difficult too. Whenever she did, she turned her mind to the Scripture passages from Proverbs that Aunt Lois had taught her. "A true friend is always loyal, and a brother is born to help in time of need," and "Hatred stirs old quarrels, but love overlooks insults."

Since Evan's arrival, he'd been in a time of need, Paige thought to herself. And she'd learned to overlook a lot of insults in the name of love. Lois had known that Evan might be a problem. Still, she had opened her home and her heart to Evan, expecting the rest of the family to do the same.

Evan needed their love all the more because he seemed so unlovable sometimes. It was difficult to understand, but Paige knew that her father and Aunt Lois were right. All she could do was offer him her love and acceptance. God would have to change his heart.

"Maybe that should be your summer project, Beth. Learning to understand my cousin Evan."

Beth rolled her eyes. "I'm not sure the summer is long enough for a project like that. I think Evan is . . ."

Paige smiled. "Just wait, Beth. If you give Evan a chance, you might find out you like him better than you thought you would."

"Uh huh," Beth nodded doubtfully.

"Gotta go." Paige jumped to her feet. "If Evan and I

get done with the garden early enough, I'll ride over for a visit."

Paige looked back at Bryan and Beth as Lady Blue galloped across the field. A smile played at the corners of her lips. If Bryan remained as friendly as he was today, the summer might be an extra special one after all.

Paige's mood dimmed considerably as she neared the house after unsaddling Lady Blue.

Mike and Ellen Bradshaw were silhouetted in the kitchen window. Mike's hands were gesturing wildly, Ellen's clasped against her chest.

Paige could hear the muffled sounds of conversation, but they ceased when she pulled open the screen door and an unoiled hinge sang out, warning of her approach.

Her mother and father wore masks of calmness when Paige entered the room.

"Hi."

"Hi," her father answered, trying to hide the emotion generated by their conversation.

Paige meandered toward the kitchen sink. "Supper started?"

"Not yet," replied her mother.

Paige glanced at the digital timepiece on the counter. *Not ready? You could set a clock by Mother's mealtimes.* Her eyebrow arched in surprise.

"Your father and I had some things to talk over. The time got away from me," Ellen explained.

"That's okay. I had brownies at the Yorks'. I'm not very hungry yet. Should I peel potatoes?"

"Paige . . ." her father began. "I think there's something we need to discuss."

The ominous tone in his voice made a sick feeling in the pit of her stomach.

"Okay." Paige pulled out a ladder-back chair and sat down, resting her elbows on the oilcloth. "What do we have to discuss?"

Ellen and Mike exchanged a glance that made a shiver dance on Paige's spine. They were too serious. Suddenly Paige was frightened.

"Mom? Dad? Does this have something to do with the man who was in the yard today?"

"I'm afraid so."

"What's going on?" Paige fought against the note of hysteria that was rising in her throat.

Mike Bradshaw pulled out the chair across from Paige and dropped heavily onto it. "That man—Mr. Gardner he calls himself—came to talk about Grandma Bradshaw."

"Grandma? But why?" Now Paige was really puzzled. The most mysterious thing about Grandma had been how she looked without her false teeth. Whatever would that strange man have to do with Grandma?

"Mr. Gardner is searching for something. He's asking that we allow him to look around the farm and open our family records to him. He wants to look at the Bradshaw family Bible—or have us look at it for him."

"Why?" Paige was dumbfounded.

"Mr. Gardner believes he is your grandmother's son."

Paige stared blankly at her father. It was as though he'd spoken in Chinese. "What?"

"Mr. Gardner believes that your Aunt Lois and I have a missing half brother. Him."

Paige squinted her eyes and stared at her father as though he'd just landed from another planet. "I don't get it."

"Gardner claims that there was a third child born to Grandma Bradshaw—an older child, from another marriage—before her marriage to Grandpa Bradshaw, who was given up for adoption before Grandma married Grandpa.

He believes he is the child from Grandma's first marriage."

"But Grandma was never married before!" Paige paused. "Was she?"

Mike sighed and shuffled his feet against the linoleum. "Not that we know of. But," and he sighed again, "Grandma did leave a few years of her life pretty much untalked about."

"The Depression," Paige supplied, familiar with the subject that had made her grandmother become anxious and sharp.

"But from what we've put together," Ellen began, "your grandmother suffered a great deal during those years—just like hundreds of people did. Hunger, poverty, homelessness. I don't blame her for not wanting to look back to that time in her life."

"He says he's your *brother*?"

"My *half* brother. And he wants your mother and I to help him prove it."

"But Grandma would have told us . . . ."

"That's what we think too, Paige. That's why we've asked this man to leave us alone. Your mother and I believe that he's a fraud."

"It's crazy, really," Paige concluded. "Grandma wouldn't give up her own child. Grandma thought babies were God's most precious miracle!" One of Paige's fondest memories was of Grandma rocking whatever child came to their house, a blissful, loving expression on her face and eyes closed in near ecstasy at having a baby in her arms.

"And anyway, what about the baby's father?" This story was getting scary. Paige was glad her father had sent the man away.

"He doesn't seem to know much about the man he claims is his father. Apparently Gardner is doing some research on that as well."

"I don't believe it," Paige announced with all the certainty a nearly sixteen-year-old can muster. "Grandma would've told us."

Mike Bradshaw shook his head. "I wish Ma were here right now to straighten things out. She'd put this Gardner fellow in his place with a glance."

Ellen and Paige chuckled in spite of themselves. They both had been on the receiving end of Grandma Bradshaw's disapproving stares. One look could wither the bravest heart.

"What does Aunt Lois think about this?"

Paige's father shrugged. "I'm not sure. We discussed it when the fellow came around right after Grandma's funeral and decided never to mention it again. She agreed that if our mother had had another child, surely he or she would have surfaced before now. After all, Grandma lived on this farm all her married life. That doesn't sound like 'running away' to me."

"Does anyone else know besides you guys and Aunt Lois?"

"No. We made the decision not to tell another soul. If he is her son, he should have come while she was alive. Not now. Not when she's gone."

Mike's eyes misted and Paige felt as though hers would too. She blinked rapidly, her eyes felt watery and itchy. She hadn't realized just how much she'd missed her Grandmother. Paige rubbed one eye with the back of her hand.

Sarah Bradshaw had been Sarah Cassidy when she met and married Benjamin Bradshaw. A slight and delicate Irish colleen, she made up in spunk and stamina what she lacked in stature. Paige sometimes wished she'd inherited her grandmother's wistful beauty instead of the solid, Scandinavian loveliness of her mother.

Paige had always felt large and gangly next to her tiny Grandmother, but Grandma made her feel delicate and graceful inside, in her heart. Eventually, Paige discovered, that confident, loved feeling in her heart translated into outward poise. Grandma Bradshaw had given her a beautiful inheritance.

Paige felt a righteous anger growing within her. "I don't understand why anyone would do this to us! Why would anyone want to hurt our family this way?"

"He's a crook, honey. A con man. That's all we can figure." Mike looked at his wife with anguish in his eyes. "That's got to be it. There's no other explanation."

Paige blinked, surprised by the current of emotion flowing between her parents. "So," she resolved, "if he's a crook, then there's nothing to it. We shouldn't be upset. Our family hasn't done anything." She paused as her mother and father turned miserable expressions on each other. "Have we?"

The slump of her father's shoulders and her mother's nervous fingers that kneaded the fabric of her apron spoke more loudly than any words.

"Well, *have* we?"

"I'm afraid there is more to this, honey. There's something he wants."

"What?" Paige was startled and frightened. What could it be? Something that was precious to her?

Paige's father inhaled deeply, his muscles straining at the buttons of his plaid flannel shirt. His shoulders squared in resolve. "He wants an inheritance."

"What?" Paige was surprised by the high-pitched squeak of her voice. She cleared her throat and asked again, "What did you say?"

"He's claiming he's the rightful recipient of one-third of your grandmother's estate."

"But he can't!" She paused. "*Can* he?"

Bradshaw sighed and raked agitated fingers through his dark hair. "Maybe. Maybe not."

"You mean that you and Aunt Lois have to give this man money?"

"No, not exactly."

Paige was becoming impatient with the push and pull quality of the conversation. Couldn't her father just *tell* her what was going on?

"We learned after your grandmother died, that she'd added a codicil to her will ten years ago. In it, she'd left one third of her estate to Lois, one third to myself and," Mike inhaled deeply, "one third of the estate is being held in trust in the event of the discovery or location of another party who might have equal claim with Lois and me to her inheritance." Paige felt as though her breath had been knocked out of her.

"We were stunned, Paige," Ellen broke in. "We'd never expected her will to be anything but straightforward. We assumed that Grandma Bradshaw," and her voice broke, "was going senile at the time. Why else would she do a thing like that?"

Everything began to fall into place. No wonder her parents and Aunt Lois had been so distressed after Grandmother's death! It had always been confusing to Paige. Her grandmother had never been afraid of dying. She knew Grandma had eagerly anticipated meeting her Lord. Paige had never understood the intensity of her family's grief.

But it wasn't Grandmother's death that had troubled them so. It was the odd circumstances of the will that had pulled them into an eddy of despair.

Paige's quick mind clasped onto her mother's words. "But Grandma wasn't senile!"

"We didn't think so, honey. But why else would she do such an odd, out-of-character thing as leave one-third of her estate to an unnamed heir?"

"Grandma wasn't senile," Paige repeated stubbornly. "She wasn't." Grandma was as quick-witted as Paige herself. Only days before her death they'd talked of Paige's future, and of Evan's. Grandma's faculties were completely normal.

"I'm sorry, Paige. I didn't want to think so either. But what other explanation did we have? Not once did my mother mention an earlier marriage, another child, *anything* that would lead us to believe Lois and I had another sibling." Mike shook his head. "It had to be in her imagination."

"The family Bible? Was anything written in the Bible?"

Mike grimaced. "That Bible came from my father's side of the family. The first recording my mother made in it was her own wedding. There's nothing about her before that."

"But that's why the stranger wanted to look at the Bible!" Paige gasped. "He wanted to see if *he* were . . ."

"In the Bible? Hardly." Her father's words were cold. "I'm sure he wanted to see that there was nothing in the Bible to prove his story false."

"And it does, all right," Ellen added. "Since your grandmother's name isn't mentioned until the date of her wedding, he could maintain that he was part of her life before that date and already removed from her life by the time she and Grandpa Bradshaw married."

"There's simply no other explanation, Paige. You know as well as any of us that your grandmother couldn't give up her own child."

It was true. Paige couldn't imagine how such a thing could be possible. But what about the stranger?

"But why is he here?"

"The money. I suppose crooks like him have ways of finding out about situations of which they may be able to take advantage. Chiselers and con men make their living doing just that. He heard of this odd situation and came to try and make the most of it."

"What *does* happen to the money?" Paige wondered,

her mind spinning with the possibilities.

"Grandma stated that if the money wasn't claimed for ten years after her death, that portion of her estate would revert to Aunt Lois and me. We decided that the remaining third of the inheritance should be divided between you and Evan, since you are the only grandchildren. It was to become your college money. It's actually a good deal more than you will need, but we know how much importance Grandma placed on a good education. We thought it would have pleased her."

"But what if . . ." she began.

"What if Mr. Gardner *is* my half brother? Paige, surely any living child of Grandma Bradshaw's with proof of his heritage would have come forth by now. That is, of course, if it even made sense that there *were* any other living children!"

"But Mr. Gardner *doesn't* have any proof. Maybe that's why he's waited so long! Maybe he needed—"

"That's enough, Paige. Don't let your imagination run away with you. This is not one of your mystery stories. This is real life. *Our* life. Gardner is a con man. We won't let him disrupt our family."

"We just thought you should know, Paige," Ellen interjected. "You're old enough to realize the implications of this. Your father has asked Mr. Gardner not to set foot on the farm again. This should be the end of it."

"But he could *never* prove himself to be your brother if you didn't let him come here and search for evidence!" Paige pointed out.

"Until I can think of a reason that Grandma Bradshaw would have a marriage and a child that she never mentioned, until I can figure out why she'd leave one-third of her estate to someone we didn't know existed, and until your mother or I discover some overwhelming piece of evidence that we've overlooked for twenty years, we are going to consider Mr. Gardner a crook and a thief. Do you understand?" Mike looked fierce.

Paige nodded. She did understand. But what about Gardner? She thought of the dejected stoop to his shoulders and the sad, beagle-like expression. He didn't *look* like a con man. Just an unhappy man.

"This is the last I want to hear of this." Mike was adamant. "We're going to act as though this distressing incident never occurred. I'm sorry you had to be told about this, Paige, but we thought you needed to know."

Paige gave her father a grateful glance. "Thanks, Daddy. I *was* pretty curious."

Mike chuckled and the grim atmosphere lightened. "You're always curious, Paige. That's both the best and worst thing about you. Your curiosity makes you interesting, *but*," and he wagged a finger in front of her nose, "curiosity killed the cat."

"Oh! That reminds me!" Paige snapped her fingers. "Beth asked me if I wanted a kitten when they're older!"

Mike and Ellen laughed. "Why not? It will take your mind off our family mystery."

Paige only smiled. Her mind wasn't off the mystery yet.

3

*T*he stranger had been on Paige's mind all day. It was odd, Paige thought, how the more she decided *not* to think about something, the more often it came popping into her mind. It was like an itch she didn't want to scratch, persistent and difficult to ignore.

She'd spent the morning mowing the lawn. With every sweep of the mower, she'd find herself looking up to see if the battered old Chevy was coasting silently into the yard. In her mind's eye, she could see the tall, sad-faced man gliding toward her, hand outstretched as though he were asking for help.

At lunchtime she could no longer ignore her questions.

"Mom, do you *really* think that Grandma was . . . senile?"

Ellen gave her a sharp warning look and then glanced at her husband's dark head. "I thought we weren't going to discuss this again, Paige."

"But I've been thinking—"

"Then you'd better quit. Thinking about that subject, I mean." Mike's voice was stern with warning. "It's a closed book, Paige. It only distresses us. We want nothing more than to believe that Grandma had all her faculties, but that doesn't seem to have been the case. We have to accept that she was becoming mixed up about some things these last years."

"She didn't seem mixed up to me."

Mike turned grieving eyes on his daughter. "Your grandmother suffered through a good many hardships during the Depression, Paige. People sometimes carry scars with them for the rest of their lives. Something from that time affected Grandma. For some reason she imagined that there was another child in her family. Wishful thinking, maybe, but we can't dwell on that. We have to think of all the good times we shared with her and not let the troubles we've faced since the funeral get in the way."

Paige nodded, but she didn't like it. Grandma *wasn't* confused or senile. She was clear-headed and lucid until the day she died. Paige didn't want her memory tarnished with mistaken notions. She sighed and stared into the bowl of broth she was eating. She'd like nothing better than to erase the shadows around Grandma's memory.

"Want to go into town with me today, Paige?" Mike offered in an obvious attempt to distract his daughter from her thoughts.

"What day is this?"

"Tuesday. The library's open."

"Sure!" Paige's spoon clattered into her bowl. "Miss Weatherby said I could have 'unlimited access' to the books in the library this summer. That means I can check out as many as I want at once!"

"Maybe we should drive the truck rather than the car," Mike observed, "in order to have room to carry all these books."

"Dad," Paige grumbled. "You know what I mean. If I think I can read seven or ten books in a week, I can bring them home, that's all."

Mike laughed, "I know, Chapter, I know. Get your jacket and we'll go."

———

Nashton, North Dakota, was little more than a village

by big city standards, but for Paige, it was home. Main Street had one of everything—one bank, one barbershop, one drugstore, one bakery, and, most important of all, one library.

Paige inhaled deeply as she stepped inside the ancient brick and marble building. There was a certain smell of old books and fresh paper. She loved it.

The stairs creaked and groaned under her weight as she mounted the steps to the library's main room. Floor-to-ceiling bookshelves flanked the walls. The librarian's desk jutted into the center of the room. To one side, some small children sat on a carpet remnant reading picture books.

"Hello, Paige," Miss Weatherby whispered.

She was as old and wrinkled as some of her books. Her skin was dry and transparent as onionskin paper. Daubs of rouge stood out on each cheek like civilized war paint. Her hands were maps of blue veins and age spots, folded primly over the blotter on her desk.

"Hi, Miss Weatherby," Paige mouthed silently. Paige even found herself whispering greetings to Miss Weatherby when they met on the street. The woman was steeped in whispers.

Paige turned immediately to the shelves she loved most. The mysteries were under a little brass sign proclaiming proudly, "MYSTERY SHELF."

Paige scanned the rows for something new, something she hadn't read. Before her dark eyes could settle on any titles, she heard a scraping noise coming from behind her. Curious, Paige cranked her head around the row of shelves to see who was browsing in the old city records.

No one ever spent time in that dark corner of the library. Oral history was all anyone ever needed in Nashton. No one seemed to move away, so every family had someone who had *lived* the history of the little place.

It took all of Paige's presence of mind to keep from crying out.

Craning her neck and shoulders around the bookshelf, she came face-to-face and eyeball-to-eyeball with the stranger. He was as startled as she.

Paige swallowed the knot of fear that had sprung into her throat. "Hello," she whispered.

"Hello," he whispered back.

Paige looked to the right and to the left. Empty. She rounded the corner to face him. "Why are you here?" Her whispered words echoed like a shout in her ears.

"I'm looking for something." He didn't seem to mind her asking.

"The same thing you were looking for at my parents' house?" she asked. The question seemed bold and brazen, but sounded weak and only mildly curious on her lips.

"Yes. Do you know about that?" His eyebrow arched in question.

"I think so. Some of it, anyway. You've upset my parents."

"I'm sorry." He seemed genuinely sad about that fact. "I was afraid that would happen."

"Then why did you come?"

He studied her for a moment, weighing his answer and measuring the amount of trust he should put in this inquisitive girl.

"Because I felt I had to."

"But why now?" she queried.

He scrutinized her again. "How much do you know?"

"I don't know, actually. Just a few things my parents told me."

"About my mother?"

Paige stiffened. "You mean *my* grandmother. Not your mother."

"She was my mother. I'm sure of it."

"Then prove it." Paige's jaw jutted forward in determination.

"I'm trying," he whispered, waving a hand toward the stacks of old records and newspapers he'd spread on a table.

Paige's eyes widened. He certainly believed the tale he was telling.

"If you two are going to be chatting, you'll have to go into the conference room!" Miss Weatherby had glided up behind them so silently that she startled them both. Paige stifled a squeak and the man clapped a hand over his mouth. Before they knew what was happening, Miss Weatherby had ushered them into the soundproof conference room and closed the door behind them.

Paige found herself staring at the dark-suited, sad-faced stranger. "Mr. Gardner?" she ventured.

"Miss Bradshaw?" he inquired.

"Paige."

"Samuel."

Paige wiped the palms of her hands on the legs of her jeans. They were beginning to perspire. Samuel Gardner gestured toward two chairs.

"Shall we sit down?"

"I'm not sure." Paige glanced at the conference room door. She was safe enough here. Miss Weatherby could hear a whisper at three hundred yards. If Paige needed to scream for help, the soundproofing wouldn't be enough to foil the librarian's acute ears. Miss Weatherby would be onto Mr. Gardner before he knew what hit him.

"I'm not dangerous, Paige. The most awful thing I'm claiming to be is your half uncle."

"Don't say that!" Paige retorted, clenching her fists against her thighs. "You aren't! You can't be! Grandma would have told us!"

"Not necessarily," he countered. "There could have been reasons for keeping my existence a secret."

"Name one." She mirrored the defiance she felt.

His face sunk into even sadder lines. "I don't know."

Paige was surprised to see tears in his eyes.

"It's a question I've asked all my life, Paige. Why? Why would a mother give up her child? Why?"

"What makes you think that my grandmother is your mother, anyway?" Paige suddenly felt sorry for the man. At least she'd had the privilege of loving and being loved by Grandma Bradshaw.

"My adoptive parents gave me the name shortly before they died. It's my only clue."

"There must be a lot of Sarah Cassidy's in this world," Paige commented. "Surely more than just my grandmother."

"Maybe. But I think she is the one I'm related to."

"Why?" Paige felt rude giving this man such a grilling, but she couldn't stop now.

"Intuition, I guess." He shrugged as if he were baffled by the question.

"Intuition and money?" Paige watched his face. It only became more sad-looking.

"I regret the money, Paige. I was almost sorry to learn that one-third of your grandmother's estate is being held in trust for an unnamed heir. Because I didn't arrive while Sarah was still alive, because your dad thinks I'm after her money, he doesn't trust me. I'm sure that's what's keeping your father from believing my story."

"When did you learn about it?"

"From your father—after the funeral." Samuel's eyes misted. "I thought I was coming to Nashton to see my mother. Instead, I was too late—all I found was a fresh grave." His voice seemed to shatter like brittle glass.

Paige felt herself softening.

"The will only makes me more sure that I am your grandmother's first child."

"My father says you're a crook and a thief." The words stung across her lips, but she had to say them. "He says that you heard about the odd circumstances of Grandma's will and came to try and take advantage of us."

"I know." Samuel didn't seem angered. "I would have felt the same way if I were him. But that's truly not why I came. I came because I wanted to discover my heritage, not an inheritance."

"My parents say that Grandma was getting confused and senile because of what she did to her will."

"Do you think that's so?" Samuel studied her closely.

Paige tried to shrug nonchalantly, but it didn't work. "No."

"Then why do you think she added that codicil to the will?"

"I don't know."

"Would you like to help me find out?"

Paige's eyes grew wide. Here it was. A real, honest-to-goodness mystery. Just like her books. There was even the requisite mysterious stranger. Her shoulders began to twitch with excitement.

"My parents might not like it."

"I wouldn't ask you to do anything that would hurt your parents."

"Your coming to the farm has already hurt them," Paige pointed out.

"I'll quit coming if you help me and you prove that I'm not your grandmother's child."

"Promise?" Paige glared at him, warning him not to lie.

"I promise. If, with your help, I don't find any sort of clue that leads me to believe that I am a relative of yours, I will leave quietly and you and your family will never hear from me again."

"What kind of clues?" Paige asked before adding, "Just in case I decide to do this."

"Birth records, a lock of baby hair, a footprint done in ink, any memento that your grandmother might have saved to prove that I existed. A letter, maybe. Or something written in the family Bible."

"You want me to look around the farm for this?"

"If you would. Your parents don't want to see me. They certainly won't let me sit in your attic and go through family mementos."

"And if I prove that there was no other child, you'll go away?"

He nodded solemnly. "I promise."

Paige thought hard about what she should do. Her parents' determination to ignore the situation had only made her more intrigued by it. But more importantly, if she were to solve this mystery, then her family could be free of this man forever. That is, of course, unless she discovered he was telling the truth. . . .

"I don't know . . ."

Suddenly, surprisingly, he changed the subject. "Are you a mystery buff?"

She nodded.

"Me too. Maybe otherwise I would never have pursued this thing any further." He smiled and the sad face brightened handsomely.

He'd struck the proper chord. Paige squared her narrow shoulders. Nancy Drew wouldn't turn a mystery down. Neither would she. They didn't come her way often. How could she resist?

"I'll look around the farm—on one condition."

"You name it."

"You never come out there and upset my parents anymore."

"It's a deal."

"And you never come near me."

"But how will we meet?"

"Here. At the library. In one month."

"Fine. One month."

"*And,*" Paige continued, "I'm going to tell two of my friends what I'm doing—just in case."

"Just in case?" Samuel Gardner looked puzzled. "Just in case what?"

"Just in case something happens to me—like in the books."

"Oh." He nodded, looking like he thought that was a very wise idea. "You *are* a mystery buff, aren't you?"

Paige was warming to her subject. "I'll keep notes of every place I look. If, in one month, you look at the list and think of places I've missed, I'll look again. If nothing turns up, you have to go away and never come back. One month. It all has to be settled in one month."

"It seems fair enough to me," Samuel agreed. He studied her admiringly. "You're a very smart girl, Paige Bradshaw. I hope you *are* my niece. I like you."

Paige felt herself blushing. "Four weeks, Mr. Gardner. That's all. I'll meet you here one month from today."

They shook hands somberly and parted.

Paige found herself two steps outside the library before she realized that she'd left without checking out any books. Red-faced, she turned around and went inside. When her father picked her up, she had an armful of new mysteries to read—and one very special one in her head to solve.

———

She was going to burst if she didn't talk to someone. Paige paced the floor of her bedroom like a caged lion. Her toe caught on the multi-hued rag rug that covered all but the outside edges of the gleaming hardwood floor. She landed in a heap at the foot of her bed.

"Paige, are you all right?" Ellen called from the bottom of the stairs.

Paige bit her lip. This was no way to begin investigating her first case.

"Fine, Mom. I just tripped."

"Well, be careful. By the way, Beth called. She wanted you to come over and make cookies with her."

"Great!" Paige shot for the stairs. She needed to talk to someone, anyone, right now.

Lady Blue gave Paige a startled look as the girl bolted into the barn. Riding bareback, her knees clutching the Arabian's sleek body, Paige and the horse galloped through the field. The wind licked Paige's straight brown hair into a frenzy. She leaned forward into the horse's neck and listened to the litany that was echoing in her head.

One month. One month. One month.

She had one month to prove Samuel Gardner was mistaken about Grandmother Bradshaw. One month to drive the man away from her home and family. One month to be the detective she'd always fantasized she was. One month. . . .

Her hands tightened on the reins. There was also one month in which to prove that Samuel Gardner *did* have some bizarre claim on her family, her life. A knot of worry tightened in Paige's throat.

She swallowed. It couldn't be. It simply couldn't be.

"Hi, Paige!" Bryan waved from the chicken coop door. He was grimy from the field and carried a bucket of feed. To Paige, he was absolutely gorgeous.

Paige closed her eyes for a moment, squelching the embarrassing thought, before returning the wave. That funny feeling in the pit of her stomach was back—the feeling she always got when Bryan noticed her.

Smart, Bradshaw, she lectured herself. *Really smart. Why wouldn't he pay attention to someone galloping into his yard like the National Guard was after her? Shape up.*

But it didn't help. She was *still* glad that Bryan had noticed.

"Well, it's about time you got here." Beth was standing in the doorway covered with flour. Even her red hair was pale with flour dust.

"I didn't know it was an emergency," Paige retorted as she tied Lady Blue's reins to the fence near enough to the grass for grazing.

"Bryan says that when I cook, it's always an emergency."

"Guess I should have thought of that." Paige grinned. Poor, disorganized Beth. Common sense was certainly not equally distributed in this family.

"Did you finish planting the garden?" Beth inquired. "With *Evan*?" Her nose turned up in a wrinkle. Paige could see the dislike in the other girl's eyes.

"No. We never even got started."

"Why? I thought that was the big project this week."

"Evan said he hurt his knee playing touch football with the guys, so Aunt Lois told us to wait until next week to put the garden in. I guess it's still early."

"*Did* he hurt his knee?" Beth asked suspiciously.

"I doubt it. But you know Aunt Lois. She's so honest that she'd never dream Evan would lie. I think he just didn't want to do it."

"You may end up putting it in by yourself."

"Maybe. Evan has weaseled his way out of work before."

"He's so . . ."

"You'd better not say it, Beth. He's my cousin, after all."

"*Adopted* cousin. At least you don't have any of his lazy genes."

Paige grinned. "My dad says I could be a Lazy Bones. Does that count?"

"You know what I mean. Evan seems to make an effort not to fit in."

Paige shrugged. "He's getting better, though. Remember when he first came to live with Aunt Lois?"

"He was like a little wild animal, hiding behind Lois or the furniture. He was scared of everyone," Beth mused.

"He'd been in more foster homes and institutions than he could remember. I think he was afraid someone would take him away from Aunt Lois, too. Now that he's gotten over that, he's much nicer."

"Well, I didn't invite you over here to talk about Evan. I don't even *like* Evan!" Beth announced. "I wanted help baking these monster cookies."

And monster cookies they were. The bowl was monstrous. The heap of batter was monstrous, and the size of each individual cookie was monstrous.

"I was thinking of putting only two or three cookies on each cookie sheet."

"That's like eating half a dozen regular-sized cookies, Beth. Are you sure?"

"Mom said I could do what I liked. Anyway, Bryan eats half a dozen no matter what size they are."

"Okay. If you say so." Paige rolled up her sleeves and washed her hands before digging both fists into the rich oatmeal, butter, and coated-candy batter.

Dozens of huge cookies were spread on the table when Bryan sauntered in from the yard.

"Smells good in here."

"Let's take a plateful and go into the family room," Beth suggested. Even her freckles had been powdered away by flour. She had a daub of brown sugar on the tip of her nose.

"Are you sure you don't want to take a bath first? You really get into your work, don't you?" Bryan teased.

Beth flipped around and stomped toward the living

room with the cookies. "Careful, or you can't have any."

"Okay," Bryan agreed as he took a stack of three cookies from the table and nodded toward Paige to bring the carton of milk. They walked together into the Yorks' family room, side by side, shoulder to shoulder. That funny feeling was back.

As they sat quietly eating, Paige's thoughts turned again to her meeting in the library. One month. Only one month to solve the mystery.

"Paige, are you okay?"

Bryan's face was near her own. His eyes were dark with concern.

"Huh? Oh, yeah." She wiped a hand across her eyes.

"You really faded out on us. What were you thinking about, anyway?"

She could see Bryan's puzzlement and Beth's curious stare.

Paige sighed and studied her friends. Her eyes traveled across the pair. Bryan leaned back in the couch and crossed his ankle over his knee. He was somber. Beth squirmed next to him, obviously wondering about her friend's odd mood. Paige made a decision.

"I have something I'd like to talk to you about."

Beth's eyes grew wide and her mouth puckered into a silent "oh."

"Sounds serious," Bryan commented.

"It is, I'm afraid. And if I tell you, you've got to promise to keep everything I say a secret."

Paige and Bryan both found themselves looking at Beth.

She plumped up like an indignant Bantam hen. "Don't look at me that way! I can keep a secret as well as the next person!" Some of her huffiness vanished. "Well, almost as well . . ."

"If I tell you this, Beth, you *can't* tell another soul. You can only talk to Bryan and me about it. But," and Paige faltered, "I think I might need your help."

"Paige, if you're in some kind of trouble, you should be going to your parents, not us." Bryan's eyes were kind.

"It's my parents that are in trouble, Bryan. I *can't* go to them."

"They're getting a divorce?" Beth gasped. "I wouldn't have thought . . ."

"No, silly!" Paige interjected. "Not *that* kind of trouble!"

Then Paige unfolded her story. Samuel Gardner. Grandmother Bradshaw. The missing proof. Her parents' attitudes. Finally, she told them of her meeting with Gardner in the library and her promise to search for clues. And one month. She only had one month.

Bryan's eyes were wide when she finished. Beth seemed frozen with surprise.

"I told him I was going to tell someone about our agreement just in case, well, in case something . . . funny . . . happened."

"Funny?" Beth chirruped.

"Not funny like 'ha ha'; funny like 'strange,' " Bryan pointed out. "I don't know if I like this, Paige."

"He's not going to come back to the farm. All I have to do is look. If I can't find any proof of another baby's existence, he'll go away and not bother us anymore. Then everything will be back to normal."

"But you have to meet him again . . ."

"You guys can come with me. Anyway, I'll need you to help me search. It's a big farm. I'll need help to look everywhere in a month without making my dad suspicious. Please?"

"I don't know, Paige. I'm still not sure I approve of this," Bryan cautioned.

"It sounds *scary* to me!" Beth exclaimed.

Bryan and Paige both turned to her and said in unison, "*Everything* sounds scary to you, Beth!"

The three laughed. Yet there was an edge of nervousness to the sound.

"Well, will you?" Paige asked.

"One month, you say?"

"That's all."

"I suppose," Bryan reluctantly agreed. "You'll do it anyway. I'd rather think I'll be around to help you if you need me."

"If Bryan will help, so will I," Beth chimed in.

"But you'll have to keep it a secret," Paige warned again, knowing full well Beth's weakness in that area.

"And you can't be running around screaming every time you get startled," Bryan added to his sister.

Beth's lower lip began to protrude. "You guys don't think I can do it. Well, I can. You just wait and see."

Solemnly, the three shook hands. "One month," they intoned together. "One month."

"So," Bryan asked, "when do we start?"

"My parents are going to their Bible study tonight. Do you want to come over? It will be a long evening because they're having a potluck supper beforehand."

"Our mom and dad said they were going to Bible study, too. Let's make pizza at your house and then we can start looking."

"Frozen pizzas. Then we'll have more time to hunt."

"I'll bring the monster cookies," Beth offered brightly. "We'll need lots of energy!"

Paige and Bryan glanced at each other over Beth's bright, bobbing head. Perhaps teaching Beth to be a sleuth was going to be more of a challenge than either of them had thought. But Paige's confidence soared when Bryan winked and curled his thumb and index finger into an "A-OK" sign.

The one thing that Paige had feared most this summer was that it would be boring. Now Samuel Gardner and Bryan York had ensured it would not.

4

"*D*on't you ever *clean* up here?" Beth's voice was muffled, coming from behind a thick blanket hanging on a wire strung between two rafters.

Paige's voice floated indignantly in reply. "Of course we do! Every fall. Don't you *dare* tell my mother we were up here and you thought it was dirty!"

"Achooo!" Beth snuffled. "Not dirty, just dusty. Achooo!"

"Owww!" The wail followed a muffled "thunk."

"Bryan? Are you all right?" Paige called.

"Just stubbed my toe on this old trunk. Does your dad have any extra hundred-watt light bulbs we could screw into these sockets? I don't think we'll get anywhere feeling our way around in the dark."

"In the kitchen, under the sink. Want me to go and get them?"

"No, I will. You look around. I think I'm better at light bulbs than mysterious missing documents, anyway." Bryan disappeared down the stairs.

"Eeeppp!"

"Beth? Beth? What happened? Beth?"

"I think I stepped on a dead body!" Beth's voice sounded quavery and far away. "And I think I'm going to faint."

"Honestly, Beth, there are no dead bodies in this attic. There are seldom any *live* bodies up here." Paige would

51

have liked to strangle her friend, but it was too dark to find her neck. And, anyway, strangling Beth would have made Paige a liar about the dead bodies.

"Well, I stepped on a body. I know I did." Beth sounded like she was about to cry.

Paige shuffled toward her friend holding the trouble-light that Bryan had found in the garage. Her own toe nudged a soft, flesh-like form.

Stifling a scream, Paige cast the light at her feet. There, fully clothed and ready for a tea party lay Miss Peggy, Paige's last childhood doll. Miss Peggy didn't seem the least put out by being trampled upon. Her plastic smile never wavered. One movable eyelid winked at Paige and Beth when the floorboard beneath her quivered.

"Miss Peggy! We used to play with her all the time!" Paige scooped the doll into her arms.

Beth emitted a weak little noise and sunk to her knees on the floor. "I thought I was going to have a heart attack."

"You're letting your imagination get the best of you," Paige announced calmly as she settled Miss Peggy against a pile of cardboard boxes. "This is only an attic, not a house of horrors."

"You never know about attics. People hide strange things in attics. I read a story once . . ."

"Don't get started, Beth. You'll scare yourself to death," Paige told her as Bryan walked in.

Both girls breathed a little sigh of relief. Even Paige was getting nervous. Between Samuel Gardner's strange story and Beth's skittishness, her own nerves were tingling.

Once Bryan screwed the bright new bulbs into the ceiling sockets, they all settled down. Paige headed for a corner of the attic.

"We should start here," she announced, "and go through everything very thoroughly. I'll draw a chart and each thing we've searched through we'll put down on the chart. That way we'll know where we've been and I'll have something to show Mr. Gardner."

"We'll never get it all done in a month," Beth announced. "It's too big a job."

It *did* seem an impossible task. The Bradshaw attic held decades worth of mementos. Every box and trunk, shelf and cranny was full. Paige sighed.

"We'll go through Grandma Bradshaw's things tonight. Tomorrow I'll tell Mom that I want to clean the attic. Going through boxes of toys and old clothes should go quickly."

"While you search all the boxes," Bryan offered, "I could be checking the structure of the house. Maybe there's a secret panel or compartment. Your grandparents lived in this house, didn't they, Paige?"

She nodded. "Grandpa and Grandma built it together."

"So she would have known if there were some convenient little hiding place to tuck things she didn't want anyone to find?"

"I suppose so. Although I can't imagine Grandma Bradshaw sneaking around hiding anything. She was so open and . . ." Paige's voice cracked.

Briskly Bryan announced, "Our folks will be home before we get anything done. Come on, girls, hurry up."

Paige felt as though she were intruding on a private life as she sorted through the mementos of her grandmother's past. A rose crushed and dried between the pages of a book of poetry. A theater ticket. A program from a summer band concert. Baby pictures of Dad and Aunt Lois.

It was as though Sarah Cassidy Bradshaw's life had started the day she'd married Grandpa Bradshaw. It was as though she were born and married at the same minute. September 22, 1939. There was no scrap of paper, no whisp of evidence that Sarah Cassidy had existed before that time.

This fact gnawed at Paige. Why? Why?

"Bleeeaaach!"

Paige dropped the photo album she was holding and stood up. Beth nearly bowled her over again in her scrambling, screaming progress across the room.

"Auuugggghhh!"

Bryan darted over to his sister. "What's wrong, Beth? Are you okay?"

Beth had posted herself on an old footstool and stood hanging onto a rafter. "There's a dead mouse back there! In a trap! *A dead mouse!*" She emphasized each word so that no one could mistake the dreadful meaning of her words.

"But, Beth," Paige pointed out calmly, "you weren't that noisy when you thought you'd found a dead body."

"I only *felt* the body. I *saw* the mouse."

"Dead bodies? You felt a dead body?" Bryan's head was pivoting from one girl to the other.

Paige held up Miss Peggy. "Dead body, all right. Dead as plastic and foam stuffing can be. Beth has an overactive imagination."

"Beth's generally overactive," Bryan said in disgust. "Her mouth, her imagination, her appetite . . ."

Beth jumped off the footstool and started to pummel her brother. They were rolling on the floor laughing when Paige silenced them. "I think I hear a car. It's our folks. Come on, let's get out of here!"

If the Bradshaws and the Yorks noticed the light smattering of dust on their children's clothing and hair, they said nothing about it. As he and Beth left with their parents, Bryan whispered to Paige, "Call me when you need me." Paige nodded.

As she turned to go to her room, she noticed a rather silly grin on her father's face. "One month, Chapter. Remember, one month."

Her eyes flew open in amazement. Did he know of her agreement with Mr. Gardner? How?

"I told you that you couldn't date until you were sixteen. That's a month away. I saw how you and Bryan were whispering. Just don't make any plans I wouldn't approve of."

"*Oh, Daddy!*" Relief and embarrassment mingled within her. Suddenly her entire life was on a time schedule. One month till Gardner promised to go away for good. One month until she was sixteen. One month until . . . Well, she couldn't predict anything about Bryan York. But she could *hope*, couldn't she?

Smiling, she went to bed.

————

"Evan is here, Paige. He's ready to start on the garden." Ellen Bradshaw's voice penetrated through the nest of blankets into which Paige had burrowed.

Paige slowly emerged from her warm cocoon of sleep. What a way to wake up in the morning. Evan.

She pulled on her oldest jeans and T-shirt, found a pair of almost-too-small tennis shoes and some grubby gym socks, and padded downstairs.

Evan was having breakfast at the kitchen table.

Paige eyed him speculatively. He was nice looking, really. It was his personality that made him unpleasant, not his appearance.

His hair was brown, the color of chestnuts. It was fine, soft hair that fell persistently into his eyes. He'd developed a habit of scraping it back from his forehead with an impatient air. Somehow, it made him look irritated and haughty.

Evan had nice, even features and pale blue eyes. He was not as tall as Bryan York or nearly so muscular. Perhaps some of that was because Evan spent a good deal of his time avoiding work, while Bryan seemed to seek it out. Evan's hands were soft and uncalloused. Bryan's were thick and hard from outdoor chores.

"Whatcha staring at?" Evan asked. His voice held a hint of a whine.

"Sorry. Was I staring? I didn't mean to be. I'm still sleepy." Paige shuffled to the table and poured corn flakes into a bowl.

"How come you get to sleep in?"

"Lucky, I guess. Did you bring the seeds?"

"Lois sent a whole bag of stuff."

Paige studied him covertly. Evan refused to call Aunt Lois "Mother." She'd tried to let him know how much it would please her, but he'd always kept that bit of distance between them. Perhaps at some time Evan *had* called someone mother and been disappointed. Anyway, Paige had never heard him call his adoptive mother anything but Lois.

Paige knew it had to hurt her aunt. Lois had never married. But it had not shocked anyone when she announced that she was planning to adopt a child, an older child, who needed mothering. Next to her own mother, Paige imagined that Aunt Lois would be one of the nicest mothers in the world.

"So what do you want to be in charge of planting?" Paige inquired.

"I'll do the corn, peas, and the potatoes. You can do the rest."

Thanks, Paige thought to herself. He'd picked all the easy stuff and left her to do the tiny seeds that took so much more time. She said an extra prayer for patience over her morning cereal. Evan did seem to be her cross to bear—Evan and Mr. Samuel Gardner.

By noon, Paige would have been willing to trade Evan for a dozen Samuel Gardners.

"What time is it, Paige?"

"Eleven forty-five. Three minutes and twenty seconds

after the last time you asked me what time it was. And six minutes and forty seconds since the time before that."

"You don't have to get nasty."

"I'm not nasty. I'm frustrated. Every time I get a rhythm going with these seeds, you have me stop and look at my watch. Mom will call us when dinner is ready, don't worry."

"I don't know how I let Lois talk me into doing this," Evan complained. "This is really boring."

Paige refrained from commenting on the sulk in her cousin's voice. "My dad *told* me I was doing this. And it's not boring. Look around you, Evan. Look at the sky. It's like a big blue canopy. And the birds, why, I look at the birds and . . ."

"Can it, Paige. What's so special about sparrows and sky?" Evan rammed the nose of his trowel into the soft black earth. "Especially when we could be playing video games."

"You'd rather be playing video games?" She was about to wind up for a big lecture when Ellen Bradshaw came to the farmhouse door and began to wave a white dish towel toward the garden.

"What's wrong with your mother? Is she surrendering?" Paige detected the sneer in his voice.

"No, silly. Lunch is ready."

"Good. I'm starved from all this work." Evan jumped up from his knees and started for the house.

"What work?" Paige muttered. Practically all Evan had done in the garden was keep her company. Not very good company, at that.

He was already washed and at the kitchen table when Paige entered the house. His hand was clutching a fork suspended mid-air over a plate of pork chops.

"Aren't you going to wait until we say grace?"

The fork wavered, then plunged into a slice of meat. "Nah, I'll just eat till you get here."

"Evan . . ." Ellen Bradshaw warned. "We give thanks *first* at this house."

Evan's eyes folded into displeased slits. "So who's thankful, anyway?"

Only Paige heard the question. Her eyes grew round with wonder. She kicked his leg with the toe of her tennis shoe as she slid into her chair. "You are," she hissed. "We *all* are."

"For what?" the boy challenged. "Pesky cousins?"

"Among other things," Paige retorted. "This food, our families, our lives."

"Maybe you're thankful," Evan whispered, his eyes darting over his shoulder to see that Ellen had not yet returned from the pantry. "I'm not."

The food stuck in Paige's throat when she tried to swallow. What had Evan meant by that? It frightened her to see someone so bitter. Did Aunt Lois know about this?

Paige hung about the kitchen after the dishes were done and her dad and Evan went to finish the garden.

"Mom?"

"Yes, dear?" Ellen's voice was vague and faraway. Paige had disturbed her thoughts.

"What's wrong with Evan?"

"Nothing that I know of. Why?"

"He's even meaner and grumpier than usual today."

"Time and patience, Paige. Time and patience."

Paige rolled her eyes. She'd be a hundred years old before time and patience had any effect on Evan!

"I don't understand it." Paige picked at the loose weave in the kitchen curtains. "If I got to live with Aunt Lois, I'd be happy. He acts like being a part of our family is a big chore."

"That's all it is, Paige. An act." Ellen came into the dining area and pulled out a chair. "Evan has had a bad life. The social worker feels that because he was rejected so often, he's learned to thwart those who reject him—by rejecting them first. If he pretends he doesn't care for someone, then he hopes the pain won't be so great if he is separated from them."

"But Lois won't reject him!"

"You know that. And I know that. But Evan doesn't believe it quite yet. Give him time. Once he realizes that he's a part of this family forever, he'll come around."

It sounded so easy when her mother said it. Putting it into practice was another matter.

Evan was saddling Lady Blue when Paige walked into the barn.

"Hey! What are you doing?" Lady Blue was hers alone. No one ever rode her but Paige.

"Your dad said I could go riding with him."

"Not on Lady Blue! You can take one of the other horses."

"I want to ride this one."

"No. She's used to me. Anyway, you're making that cinch too tight." She reached to catch Evan's hand.

Evan pushed her as she neared him. "Get out of my way, dummy. I have as much right to this horse as you do!"

Paige bit back the angry answer that brimmed on her lips. She wouldn't feel any better if she said it. Patiently she stated, "No, Evan. You can't ride that horse."

Resentment flared in the boy's eyes. He took a step toward her and shoved Paige hard against the rough board of the stall. "I can do whatever I please."

Paige felt the head of a nail scrape across her back and tears spring to her eyes. She sank gratefully to the soft hay when she heard her father's voice.

"Get away from the horse, Evan." Mike was angry. Paige could tell. His voice had a timbre that would have sent chills through a snowman.

But not Evan. Belligerently, the boy squared off against

his uncle. "She doesn't need to ride this horse all the time."

"It's her horse."

"How come Paige gets everything?"

"She paid for Lady Blue with her own money, Evan." Mike was advancing slowly toward the boy. "She worked hard for that horse."

Paige gasped as Evan snapped the tips of the crop he was holding against the mare's smooth flank. Lady Blue started and whinnied, unaccustomed to such treatment.

Before she knew what had happened, Mike had Evan by the shoulders and was ushering him out of the barn.

"I think we'd better go and talk to Lois about this, Evan. You've got some explaining to do." Mike's voice faded as he forcibly led the boy toward the pickup. The last words that Paige caught were, "You aren't welcome on this farm again until you . . ."

As Lady Blue nudged Paige's shoulder, the tears came. Anger and resentment welled in her like a bitter flood. She wanted to strike back. She wanted to hurt Evan just as he'd hurt her. Instead, a litany of love echoed in her mind.

Forgive him. Forgive him. Seventy times seven. Forgive him.

She scrubbed away her tears with the back of her hand and rose to her feet. She removed the little mare's saddle and gave her an extra ration of feed.

As Paige walked toward the house, she kicked angrily at the pebbles spotting the gravel driveway. "An eye for an eye. . ." That was in the Bible too. At the moment a little good old-fashioned retaliation would feel mighty good. "A tooth for a tooth. . ." Paige felt like yanking out one of Evan's right now.

"Paige?" Her father had already returned.

It hadn't taken long at Aunt Lois's, she thought bitterly. She met her father's anguished eyes.

"I'm so sorry."

That was enough to shatter the dam of bravery she'd been building. Paige ran into her father's arms and bawled like a baby.

Once the torrent subsided, Mike pushed her away from himself, placed his work-roughened palms against her cheeks, and wiped away her tears with his thumbs.

"Why does he do things like that, Daddy?"

"I don't know, Chapter. I really don't know. All we can do is love him and hope he'll learn to love us back."

She could feel the blood dripping between her shoulder blades from the scratch on her back. "Sometimes I just hate him, Dad!"

"I know, Paige. But we can't. Think about all the things for which Jesus has forgiven us."

"But that's different . . ." she began, before realizing that it wasn't so very different after all.

Her father smiled. "You and I both know better than that." He sighed. "And Evan has been forbidden to come to the farm without Aunt Lois for the next month. If he can't behave, he can't be here. Maybe by then, he'll have come to his senses."

Paige felt slightly cheered by the news. At least Evan wouldn't be underfoot when she and the Yorks searched for clues to Mr. Gardner's identity. Maybe the skirmish in the barn wasn't all bad after all.

"And," Mike went on, "he's writing you a letter of apology. He was sobbing by the time we got to Lois's. He's one disturbed child, Paige. Remember that."

She nodded. She couldn't even imagine what it would be like to have been tossed from one foster home to another. Maybe her mother was right. Evan made people hate him so that parting from them wouldn't be so painful. She'd fix him. She wouldn't hate him no matter how hard he worked at it!

Feeling better, Paige followed her father into the house.

———

"Beth called," Ellen announced as Paige walked through the door. "What is that child up to now?"

A sinking feeling settled in Paige's stomach. Was Beth already giving away their secret?

"Why? What did she say?" Paige struggled to be nonchalant.

"Nothing special. It's not what she said, it's *how* she said it!"

"Huh?" Paige's face crumpled in confusion. "What is *that* supposed to mean?"

"She refused to talk above a whisper, like there was someone eavesdropping on the phone."

Paige rolled her eyes.

"And she wanted to know if I knew where you were."

"What's so funny about that?"

"Well, nothing. Except," and Ellen furrowed her brow, "she went on to say, 'Do you know what she's doing? *Really doing?*' "

Paige grimaced.

"What do you suppose she meant by that?" Ellen stood, hands on her hips, looking puzzled.

"Who knows with Beth!" Paige answered honestly. She had a pretty good idea that her little red-haired friend had spent the morning reading Bryan's mystery books and was ready to reenact every one of them. Whispered telephone calls! Crazy Beth. What next?

They'd better find some clues or prove that Mr. Gardner's claims were false—and soon. Beth was the weak link in the chain. It was inevitable that she would give them away—the only question was when. She and Bryan had better hurry.

"You didn't happen to talk to Bryan, did you?" It was difficult to make the question come out casually.

Ellen glanced up with a sly smile on her face. "As a matter of fact, I did."

Paige's heart did a little flip-flop. More casually than she felt, she asked, "What did he want?"

"He was wondering if you wanted company tonight while your dad and I go with his parents to the auction sale in town. Otherwise, you kids can ride along."

"I guess I'd rather stay home," Paige shrugged, trying to look nonchalant. Another opportunity to explore!

"That's what he and Beth had decided. I told them to come over for supper. I'll put chili in the crockpot and you kids can eat whenever you get hungry. Sound okay?"

"Sounds great." Paige wondered to herself if a person could explode inside and not have it show on the outside. She was sure some of her vital organs were about to burst with excitement. Time to search! With Bryan! Oh, yes, and Beth. . . .

"Just don't make a mess anywhere," Ellen warned. "There's too much work to do around this place as it is."

"Maybe we could be outside," Paige ventured. "Like in the bunkhouse . . ."

"I can't imagine what you'd find to do in that dusty old place, but go ahead. You can't do any damage out there." Ellen wiped her hands on her apron.

"Oh, and Mom," Paige continued, "I could help you by cleaning the attic. Dust and stuff. You know." She watched her mother from the corner of her eye.

Ellen looked rather pleased. Her eyes sparkled as she turned to her daughter. "How nice of you to offer! That would help me out a great deal. Thanks, dear. It's nice to see that you're growing up!"

Paige felt a little deceitful, but she *would* clean the attic. She'd do a better job than anyone had ever done before. She'd please and surprise her mother. And if she happened to run into some old papers that were of interest—to herself or anyone else—well, that would just be an extra added bonus.

She smiled. But first things first. Now she had to go upstairs and wash her hair. Bryan was coming over tonight.

And . . . she'd almost forgotten, they were going to search the bunkhouse.

5

$\mathcal{P}$aige had her nose buried in a library book when Bryan and Beth arrived. She knew it was them without looking out the window. Beth was chattering like a magpie and Bryan was answering her with noncommittal grunts.

A person simply couldn't answer all of Beth York's questions with regular full-sentence replies. No other living tongue could talk as fast as Beth's.

Paige quickly smoothed her hair. It cascaded around her shoulders like a cloud of multi-hued silk. The strands on top were lightening to a warm honey in the summer sun. Her hair at the base of her neck was darker, like brown velvet. Her cheeks were peachy, her complexion the color of ivory silk.

She had even dressed up for the occasion—sort of. Her jeans were old, as were her tennis shoes. She'd clipped the tags from the new jean shirt in her closet and pulled it on. She'd even worn the tiny pearl earrings that her parents had given her for Christmas. It was as dressed up as she dared get to go crawling through the bunkhouse.

If, she thought to herself, she were any more dressed up, Beth would wonder why. If Beth wondered, then Bryan might wonder. And if Bryan wondered, then he might figure out that she was dressed up for him. And if he figured *that* out, then she'd be embarrassed. But if he didn't figure that out, then she'd be disappointed. . . .

She shook her head. It was all much too complicated to

consider. Anyway, Beth was already in the house.

"Paige? Are you in here? Paige? Are you all right?" Beth's voice was escalating. "Paige? Are you hurt? Bryan, she's not answering . . ."

"Hullo, Beth. I'm alive and well. I was in the living room." Paige sauntered toward her friend.

"Oh! You scared me! I thought you might be . . ." Beth paused theatrically, giving Paige the opportunity to imagine all sorts of dire events that could have overtaken her.

"She's making me crazy, Paige. We've got to get this search over with soon!" Bryan came behind his sister, pulling at the tips of his auburn hair and making distressed faces. "She thinks everything is mysterious, dangerous, spooky, or weird. She wanted me to taste test her food at dinner tonight just in case someone had gotten into it with a vial of poison."

Beth didn't even appear embarrassed. "Well, you can't be too careful . . ."

"Or too weird," Bryan added in disgust. "Who'd ever think their own *mother* might poison their food?"

"Speaking of weird . . ." Beth faced off against her brother.

"Now quit it, you two." Paige suppressed her laughter. She loved Beth when she was this way, but everything had its limits.

"Let's make a pact never to allow her to read another mystery novel when all of this is finished," Bryan pleaded.

"I thought you hated mystery stories, Beth." Paige turned to her friend.

"I did. But if you're going to solve a mystery, you need to do some *research*. I've read three really scary stories already. And I've got lots of ideas as to where the papers concerning Mr. Gardner might be. I think the hidden walkway is the best place to start."

"We don't have a hidden walkway on this farm, Beth."

Paige summoned all her patience.

"You don't know that. It's probably hidden." Beth sounded perfectly serious.

Paige swallowed. Even she was getting wrapped up in Beth's contorted logic. They'd better get into the bunkhouse before Beth had them looking for Egyptian mummies in the basement.

Beth's questions to Bryan floated to Paige's ears as they walked toward the ramshackled old building that used to house the farm's hired men. "Have you read any stories about how the great pyramids came to be?"

Paige slapped the palms of her hands to her cheeks. It was going to be a long night if that was the kind of "research" Beth had been doing!

———

The bunkhouse was the original family dwelling on the farm. Paige's grandfather had built it when he was single and lived in it for several years before he and Grandma built the big house.

There were only two rooms on the first floor and a loft upstairs that one reached by climbing a nearly perpendicular stairway. The stairway was built steeply to preserve space. It was like climbing straight up a ladder to get to the second floor.

Paige remembered her grandmother talking about cooking in the bunkhouse while the big house was being built. She'd had a potbellied stove with a flat space on top— room enough for one kettle. Apparently, Grandpa hadn't been much of a cook before he married. When Grandma came to live with him, he had had one of everything—one kettle, one plate, one knife, fork, and spoon.

Grandma had claimed she'd made a civilized man of him. Paige believed it.

"This is worse than the attic!" complained Beth again,

turning up her nose at the dust.

"No one has lived here in years," Paige reminded her.

"No wonder." Beth ran an exploratory finger across the top of the cold stove. "Urrrggh."

"Don't start making those noises, again, Beth. You have more sounds in your vocabulary than you do words," Bryan scolded his sister.

Beth flipped her red ponytail and turned haughtily away from her brother. Paige wondered how she could take him so much for granted. Bryan York was simply too special for that.

"What's this junk on the walls?"

"Oilcloth. Like the stuff you can buy in the five and dime to use as tablecloths."

"Why is it on the walls?" Beth had her nose pressed close to a sheet of blue and white checked oilcloth.

"I don't know. It was probably all they had to decorate with. It's hung up there for seventy years."

"Blech. Think of what must be behind it." Beth crinkled her nose in distaste.

"Hey!" Bryan interjected. "Good idea, Beth. Maybe something has been slipped behind the oilcloth. If we feel for any ridges in the surface of the wall that might outline a packet of papers . . ." He ran his hands along the wall. Then his shoulders slumped in disappointment. "This wall is all ridges. We'd never be able to tell a packet of papers from the lumps and bumps on the wall."

"Maybe we should start in the other room," Paige suggested brightly. "The walls in there are just plain wood."

The three of them crept into the sleeping room of the bunkhouse. The floor, which waved and rolled like the ocean beneath their feet, sang out with a melody of squeaks and groans that drowned out even Beth's odd noises.

"What's that?" Beth hissed, pointing to a tall black figure lurking in the corner behind the door.

"A pump organ. Want to hear?" Paige strode toward the curlicued affair and blew away a layer of dust.

"Let's search first and play later." Bryan's voice came from behind a bookcase.

The girls nodded in agreement. This was not the nicest place in the world to be.

An old oxen yoke hung from two nails hammered into the wall. An antique clock that had poised its hands at midnight for a dozen years hung next to a battered frying pan.

Paige noticed that a stack of burlap sacks scritched and chirruped a bit as her toe nudged the heap. Anxiously she looked toward Beth. She hadn't heard. Paige had a feeling live mice would affect Beth even more adversely than a dead one.

The three spoke little as they methodically searched every nook and cranny of the room. Bryan sighed as he leafed through the last of the musty volumes on the bookshelf.

"I don't think there's anything in here."

"I think you're right," Beth agreed, blowing a stray strand of hair from her eyes.

"We haven't looked in the closet yet," Paige offered hopefully.

"Closet? Where's the closet?" Bryan's eyes scanned the room.

"Here. It's hidden." Paige outlined the closet door set into the wall of wainscoting. Its outline followed the crevices of the wood, making it difficult to see unless one knew it was there.

"A secret walkway!" Beth announced delightedly.

"Hardly. You can't go far in a closet." Bryan toned down his sister's enthusiasm.

"It's close, isn't it, Paige?" Beth turned an injured expression toward her friend.

"Close enough. Shall we open it?"

"Let me! Let me! I want to say I discovered a secret walkway!" Beth hurried toward the door. Paige and Bryan followed behind. They stood at her shoulder as she tugged at the time-sealed doorway.

It came open with a jerk.

A puff of dust filtered down upon them.

A bloodcurdling shriek rent the air.

Clawing and gasping, Beth fought her way behind Paige and Bryan, terrified sounds spewing from her twisted lips.

Paige heard a gurgle deep in Bryan's chest.

"Sorry, guys. I forgot to tell you about the bird."

"The bird?" Bryan had regained some of his composure. Beth had recaptured none of hers.

"It's a great horned owl. My grandfather shot it and had it stuffed over fifty years ago. I forgot that my dad put it in here. It's kind of scary if you aren't expecting it," Paige explained.

The breath that Bryan expelled agreed with her more than words ever could.

"You *knew* about that thing?" Beth's shrill voice reached new heights.

The three of them stood studying the creature. It was a magnificent specimen—as stuffed birds go. Its wingspan filled the doorway and beyond. Mike Bradshaw must have tipped it sideways to get it in the closet.

The bird was awesome. Its body was nearly two feet in length, and the wingspan was more than double that. It was a fierce and formidable looking creature with its wild yellow eyes and clenched talons. It glared from the closet like an angry savage. Paige could understand why her grandfather had had it mounted.

Beth shuddered. "I'm going to search someplace else. That thing nearly gave me heart failure."

"That's what happens when you look for hidden walkways," Bryan pointed out. Still, he cast a wary eye at the winged creature in the closet.

"It's okay. I think we're done in here anyway. Maybe we'll get this whole place searched tonight." Paige sounded eager. "I'm going to work on the attic for Mom. I can finish looking up there anytime I want. Come on."

She led them up the ladder-like steps to the second story. The floor dipped deeply in the middle, causing Paige to wonder what kind of support beams her grandfather had settled on to keep the building standing. Then she shrugged. It was not likely to cave in tonight—she hoped.

"At least there's not as much junk to go through up here," Bryan commented. "Good thing, too. It's going to be getting dark soon."

Paige glanced around the room. A bed without a mattress stood in one corner. A punching bag was nailed to the sloping ceiling on the other side of the room.

"What's that for?" Beth pointed to the airless bag.

"A punching bag. Dad used to work out with it. It's all covered with spider webs now."

"And what's that big thing?" Bryan wondered, pointing at an ornate bookshelf and desk in the corner.

"A secretary. At least that's what they're called. It was Great-grandmother's. My grandma used it, too. It's really too pretty to be stuck up here. I should have Dad take it down and put it in my room."

"You should have your dad look at this window, too, Paige. It's broken. It won't matter so much now, but when the snow sifts in, it could be a real mess."

Beth had been silent for a while. Bryan and Paige noticed the quiet at the same time. They turned to see her in the dark recess of the room opposite the window squinting at an ancient picture hung on the wall.

"Who's this?" She pointed an inquisitive finger at the stern-faced man in the photo. As she pointed, her hand brushed at a drooping piece of oilcloth hanging from the ceiling.

The next horrible moments were sealed in Paige's mind in slow motion.

A flutter of wings battered the oilcloth. With lightning speed, a tiny winged creature with bright pin-prick eyes careened from the dark cavern under the eaves.

Beth screamed a piercing, terrified shriek and threw her arms across her face as the bat darted from its hiding place and into the room.

Bryan lunged for an old broom leaning against the wall and swatted at the startled creature winging its way about the room. Dealing a death-blow to the sharp-featured rodent, Bryan then swept the tiny carcass into the corner of the room.

Turning to the girls he announced, "There. That takes care of that."

But no one was listening. Paige was kneeling on the floor, fanning a dusty magazine across Beth's face. This time she had fainted dead away.

───────

"Are you better yet, Beth?"

"Can you see us all right?"

"Can you hear us?"

"Are you going to throw up?"

Bryan and Paige leaned over the girl lying on the couch. Bryan had carried his sister to the house and Paige had made a compress of cold towels to lay on her forehead. The two peered into her face like worried old scribes.

"I hate bats." The words sounded faint and far away, as though she were speaking from the bottom of a well or the far end of a tunnel. At least she was conscious.

"So it seems." Paige had a hard time keeping the laughter from her voice now that she was no longer afraid.

"I don't think I like mysteries very well." Beth's voice was drawing a little nearer, as though she were halfway through the tunnel.

"You just don't like dust or stuffed birds or bats," Bryan pointed out. "We haven't done much about the mystery yet."

Beth groaned and cautiously moved her head. "I'm not sure I can live through solving an entire mystery."

Paige grinned. "Supper will help. You'll feel better after you have something to eat."

"I can't eat like this," Beth complained. "I've got more dirt on me than a plowed field."

"I'll run a bath," Paige announced.

"Ah, Paige," Bryan stammered. "I could use a shower myself."

Paige studied him. He was right. He was coated with the pale powdery dust that sealed places seem to collect. Even his burnished copper hair looked grayed and dull.

Then she glanced down at herself. Streaks and smudges of dirt covered the front of her new jean shirt. Fortunately, the big house had three bathrooms.

———

They met at the dining room table. Beads of water glistened from Bryan's curls. Beth reminded Paige of a tiny drowned rat, with her hair slicked tightly against her head.

But Paige thought better of mentioning it. They'd all had enough of owls—and mice—and bats—for one night.

She'd changed her own clothes and run Beth and Bryan's through the rinse cycle of her mother's washing machine. They were tumbling in the dryer, the metal snaps of Bryan's jeans making clicking noises against the inside of the drum. Both he and Beth looked vaguely unhappy wrapped in Mike and Ellen's bathrobes.

"Maybe this isn't such a good idea after all, Paige,"

Bryan began as he shifted the shoulders of the red-and-navy striped robe.

"Yeah!" Beth agreed. "I don't think I can take any more bad scares!" She looked like a leprechaun swathed in Ellen's bright green robe.

"But I promised!" Paige wailed. "I'll have to do it alone if you don't help me!"

"You could get Evan to help you," Beth suggested with little enthusiasm.

Bryan and Paige both spun to face her. "Evan?" They yelped. "No way!"

Paige slumped against the kitchen table. "I wish Evan would try—even just a little bit—to be nice. Then he *could* help us. But," and she bit back the story about the Lady Blue incident, "I guess he's got to make the first move and trust us."

She'd seen him riding his little motorbike on the country road past their mailbox when she'd gone for the mail. He hadn't come onto the place since his encounter with her father. Even Evan knew it was unwise to cross Mike Bradshaw.

Still, Paige didn't like him skulking around the outskirts of the farm like that. It gave her a creepy feeling—like she was being watched. *But,* she thought to herself, *he probably was just sorry he'd been so mean. Maybe Dad was right to teach him a lesson.*

"Is it really worth it, Paige?" Bryan gave her a piercing look. His eyes were kind, but curious.

"I promised the stranger," she repeated stubbornly for the hundredth time.

"But is that so very important?"

She'd asked herself the same thing. Aloud, she said, "I think it is. If he really is family, then he has a right to the inheritance. And if he isn't, he should go away and never come back. Mom and Dad refuse to give him the benefit of the doubt."

"And maybe they're right," Bryan observed.

"But what if they're not? I promised Mr. Gardner I'd look. If I didn't find anything, he said he'd leave. I have to keep my promise."

Bryan's shoulders sagged under the big robe. He obviously could sense Paige's determination.

"Paige?" Beth's voice was smaller and more hesitant than usual.

"What?"

"What if Mr. Gardner isn't only lying?"

"Huh?" Paige's expression went blank.

"What if Mr. Gardner is . . ." and Beth swallowed hard, "dangerous?"

"There you go again, Beth, being scared of . . ." Paige began, but she didn't like the warning bell that rang in her head. Maybe, for once, Beth had a valid point. Bryan only reinforced the notion.

"I think she's right, Paige. We don't know anything about him. What if he wanted to . . ." and Bryan hesitated, considering the possibilities, "hurt you."

Paige thrust out her lower lip and gave a gusty sigh, blowing a stray strand of hair from her eyes. "I've thought of that."

"You have?" The other two echoed together.

"That's why I asked you guys to help me out. Just in case . . ." she paused. "Well, just in case."

Bryan and Beth exchanged a somber look. Finally Bryan spoke.

"I suppose we don't have much choice then."

Beth nodded grimly in agreement.

Paige felt a flood of gratitude surge through her. These were true friends. Impulsively, she put out her hands and grasped Bryan's. "Thanks. Thanks a lot."

Suddenly she felt a little silly. Mr. Gardner and the mystery had spun completely out of her mind when Bryan gave her own small hands a squeeze. She found herself thinking about the work callouses on the palms of his hands and the warmth of his skin. She thought to herself she would *like* holding hands with Bryan.

But he brought her abruptly back to the present.

"Are my clothes done?" Bryan asked. "I think I hear a car in the driveway!"

A comic scramble ensued to get the nearly dry clothing from the machine. Bryan shot for the bathroom to change and Beth jerked her jeans on under Ellen's robe.

By the time the Bradshaws and the Yorks made their way into the kitchen, all three sleuths were sitting nonchalantly at the table.

If either set of parents wondered at their children's slightly damp hair, or suspiciously moist clothing, or the blatantly innocent expressions on their faces, no one commented.

"Hi, kids. How was the chili?" Ellen inquired as she tossed her sweater over the back of a chair.

"Chili!" the three chorused.

Paige came to the rescue. "We were just going to eat it, Mom. Now you and the Yorks can join us."

"Now? This late? What have you kids been up to that made you forget about eating supper until now?"

Beth, showing more presence of mind than usual, said, "Paige showed us the big stuffed owl in your bunkhouse."

"And the punching bag," Bryan chimed.

Mike laughed. "What kids find interesting! Anything else?"

Paige added, "I think there's a nest of mice living in those grain sacks in the sleeping room, Dad. There was some funny scrambling going on in there."

The color drained from Beth's already pale features.

"You didn't tell me that, Paige Bradshaw!"

"Did you want to know?" Paige inquired.

"No! No! No!"

"Well, then . . ."

"Fine friend you are, keeping secrets . . ." Beth's tirade sputtered into a giggle.

Just then Ellen came from the pantry with a stack of bowls. "How about some chili, everyone?"

All but the spicy broth and thick chunks of beef were forgotten as the two families shared their meal together.

Bryan was the last one out of the house as the Yorks made their departure.

"Take care of yourself, Paige," he warned. His eyes looked dark and serious in the dim shadows of the porch light.

"And you take care of me too," she joked, feeling more grim than she sounded.

"I'll try."

The tips of their fingers brushed lightly together and a warm, trembly feeling climbed Paige's arm. She waved as Bryan climbed into the York car. She stood at the foot of the driveway until she could only see the diminishing headlights bouncing down the gravel road.

Paige sighed. Was he so kind because she was his sister's best friend? Because she'd committed herself to this crazy, impulsive search? Or because . . .

Her mind spinning with the possibilities, Paige went to bed.

———

"Paige! Paige! Wake up!"

"Mmmmffftt. . . ."

Her mother was ruining her dream. A perfectly good dream it was, too. Bryan was in it. Paige burrowed deeper into the covers.

"Paige Ellen Bradshaw, you get up this minute or I'm going to get the toothbrush glass!"

The toothbrush glass! Paige bolted out of bed like a rocket.

Ellen's pretty face broke into a smile. "Works every time, doesn't it?"

"Aw, Mom!" Paige complained, but she didn't take any chances by crawling back into bed.

One particularly cozy morning, Paige had not responded to her alarm clock, her father pounding on the ceiling below her room with a broom handle, or her mother's three trips to her bedroom to shake her. Finally, in desperation, Ellen had gone to the bathroom and filled Paige's toothbrush glass with ice water. When Paige still did not rouse to her mother's coaxing, Ellen had dumped the water on her. Not only did she wake up, she had to hurry to get her bedding dry before the school bus came. Paige never took any chances with the toothbrush glass again.

"Why can't I sleep in today?" she inquired, stretching lazily, like a cat in the sun.

"Too much to do. I've got bread rising, pies to make, this entire house to straighten and, if I remember correctly, you promised to clean the attic."

Paige rolled her eyes. She wondered if Mr. Gardner had any idea what he'd gotten her into.

"Are you making buns?" Paige asked as she slipped into a pair of heather-colored shorts and a waist-skimming white T-shirt.

"I suppose. And a few caramel rolls."

"Can I take some to Mrs. Smead? She can't chew very well and she loves your buns."

"I think that's a lovely idea, Paige. I'm so pleased at the way you've befriended Mrs. Smead. Poor thing. I wonder if anyone but you ever goes to visit her."

"Not often. But I like her."

Grandma Bradshaw had first introduced Paige to Mrs. Smead before Paige could remember. The two women had been young girls together back in Minnesota—friends like she and Beth were today. Mrs. Smead was nearly blind now and lived alone in the ramshackled farmstead down the road.

She was confused and wild-eyed some days and lucid on others. The poor woman frightened off well-meaning visitors with her wild talk. But Paige knew she was lonesome so she would sit for hours listening to the confused ramblings of her grandmother's old friend, knowing that everyone—even Mrs. Smead—needed someone.

"Your grandmother would be pleased to know you still visit her, Paige."

Paige curled herself onto the corner of the bed. "I think of that sometimes, but mostly I think of that verse in Matthew, the one about, 'As you did it to one of the least of these my brethren, you did it to me.'" She glanced up at her mother. "I think Mrs. Smead must be one of the 'least' Jesus was talking about, don't you?"

Ellen's eyes blurred with tears. "I think you're right, Paige." She wiped away a tear before adding, "And I think you've got your priorities straight. You help me with the bread and take it to Mrs. Smead while it's still warm—with some of that jelly we canned. The attic will wait until you get back."

Paige nodded, her heart winging with anticipation as it always did when she thought of visiting the old woman.

6

*T*he house resembled a series of weathered Popsicle sticks hung together by rusty nails. The whole structure tilted precariously toward the south, as if it had given way under a brisk northern gale. The upstairs windows were broken out and stuffed with dirty rags and old newspapers. The grass was long and ragged and the trees gnarled and old.

The barn hadn't been used for twenty or more years. It hung low in the middle, like a swaybacked horse. Its glass-less windows stared with vacant eyes onto the sprouting fields of wheat.

Paige grimaced as she tied Lady Blue to the fence post. The barbed wire was long gone, rolled away by some thief. Mrs. Smead had been alone at the house for nearly fifteen years, since her husband died. Childless, without relatives, and possessing few friends, the old woman existed in near poverty.

Mike and Ellen Bradshaw had been quietly paying her fuel and light bills for some winters now. Most of the time the old woman didn't even realize that she was not being billed for the services. If she had, her pride might have kept her from accepting their generous gesture.

Paige stepped gingerly through the front entry. The floorboards were laid only inches off the ground and moisture had rotted the wood. It felt as though it would give way beneath her feet.

The entire east side of the house seemed to shake as Paige knocked on the door.

"Who is it?" The voice was half cackle, half plea.

"It's me, Mrs. Smead, Paige."

"Paige? Is that you? Is your grandma with you?"

Paige bit her lip. Today was not a good day to visit. Mrs. Smead was living in the past. Undaunted, she pushed her way inside.

Mrs. Smead had pulled in from the edges of her house until she was doing all her living in the kitchen. A cookstove stood unused in one corner, a hand pump and dish basin in another. Dirty dishes littered the table. She slept on a daybed in the far corner. Only a shiny metallic radio gave clue that Paige had not stepped thirty years into the past.

"Where's your grandma?" Mrs. Smead squinted past Paige to the open door.

Walking calmly to the old woman, Paige took her gnarled hand and enunciated loudly into her ear. "Grandma died a year ago, Mrs. Smead. Don't you remember?"

The head of thin gray hair bobbed. "That's right. Shame on her, leaving me like that. Everyone I love leaves me."

"I won't leave you," Paige offered, touched by the lonely echo of the woman's voice.

Mrs. Smead's eyes cleared. For the moment she became lucid. "I believe you won't, deary. You're my best friend now. Just like your grandma was before you."

"And I brought you a treat," Paige offered. "Buns. A dozen of them. Fresh from the oven. And three caramel rolls. And plum jelly. Are you hungry?"

As she watched Mrs. Smead gobble down the offerings, Paige wondered how long it had been since the wizened old woman had eaten a decent meal. Silently, Paige vowed to make sure that no more than a week would pass before she returned to check on her neighbor.

"Mrs. Smead," the girl began.

"Huh?" Mrs. Smead looked at her with blurred eyes.

"Do you cook for yourself?"

"Some days, yes. Some days, no."

"Would you mind if I brought you some of my cooking? I make wonderful brownies. And I can make beef stew. Do you like beef stew?"

The woman's face suddenly became wise and alert. "Is this charity? 'Cause if it is, I don't want any."

Paige gave a snort. "Charity! I want to show off my cooking and you call it charity! Don't hurt my feelings, Mrs. Smead!"

The little woman relaxed. "Well, if you say it like that . . ." Her eyes faded in remembrance. "I used to love beef stew . . ."

Nonchalantly, so she wouldn't bring attention to herself or what she was doing, Paige began to pick up around the cluttered kitchen. Mrs. Smead had finished all three caramel rolls and was daintily licking her fingers.

Paige turned to wash the dishes she'd collected and gave a startled gasp when the sharp voice came from behind her.

"Look out! You'll fall!"

A dish clattered into the pan and shattered as Paige spun around.

Mrs. Smead was sitting bolt upright on the bed, staring into space. "Sarah Ryan, you've got to be more careful! You can't *do* things like that anymore!"

Mrs. Smead was talking to a ghost, someone from her past. Sarah Ryan? Who was that? Gently, Paige sat down next to the old woman. Taking her hand, she prodded, "Can't do things like what anymore?"

The pale eyes turned on Paige. "Sarah? Is that you? It looks like you. It must be! For a moment I thought I was dreaming." Mrs. Smead's shoulders drooped. "I dream a lot lately."

"Sarah who? Who do you think I am?" Paige persisted.

"Sarah Ryan, of course." Mrs. Smead chuckled. "I have to keep calling you that in order to get used to it. Sarah Ryan. Sarah Ryan. That's almost as pretty a name as Sarah Cassidy was. Sarah Ryan."

It took all of Paige's presence of mind not to grab the dear lady by the shoulders and shake her. What did she mean? Who was Sarah Ryan? What did she have to do with her grandmother Sarah Cassidy Bradshaw?

Suddenly, the old woman began to whimper. "I'm tired, Sarah. I'm so tired. Can I sleep now?"

Gently, Paige eased the old woman down on her bed. Her mind was spinning. What did this mean?

Regretfully, Paige left the Smead house. Mrs. Smead was fast asleep, the dishes done, the house tidied up. There was nothing more to be done or learned today, but she would go back. Perhaps her friend's mind would be clearer tomorrow. Then she could learn who this Sarah Ryan was.

But it was not to be. At least not today, Paige concluded, as she scrubbed at a grease spot on the kitchen floor. Her mother had decided she should make up for the day off by doing double duty. Aunt Lois and Evan were coming by this afternoon. Ellen wanted everything in place by then.

Evan had not been on the farm since her father banished him. Paige had seen him often, however, as close to the farmstead as he could get and still be on Aunt Lois's land. Paige wondered if he'd been sneaking around the buildings. It would be easy to go into the barn unseen. Then she felt guilty for her suspicions. Maybe he was simply sorry he'd been so mean.

If he was, he certainly didn't act like it, Paige decided

about four minutes into his visit. When Lois turned her back, he made faces at her and mouthed words that Paige didn't even attempt to decipher.

It made Paige cringe to see how hard her aunt tried to be kind to the boy—and how little he seemed to care for the attention.

"Evan has lots of projects going this summer, don't you, Evan?" Lois turned hopefully to the boy.

A gutteral grunt was his reply.

"What sort of projects?" Ellen made a stab at conversation.

"Nothin'."

"Oh, he's been cleaning out the culverts along the roads, for one thing. It's a big job."

So that was why Evan always seemed to be lurking around the farmstead! It made Paige a little less uneasy to have a reason for his presence. The memory of their scene in the barn still stung in her mind.

Lois and Ellen sent the two of them to Lois's car to carry in several sacks of quilt pieces. Paige found herself at a loss for words with her cousin. There was actually malice in his eyes. Evan hated her. Desperately, she wished she knew why, but the more she tried to talk to him, the more silent he became.

It was a relief to see her aunt and the boy drive away.

"That child is a real worry," Ellen commented as the car disappeared from sight.

"A pain in the neck, you mean."

Ellen hid a grin. "Maybe. But a worry, too. He seems to be regressing lately. He hasn't been this surly and out of sorts since the first day he arrived at Lois's. I wonder what's wrong."

Paige didn't know and didn't care to take time to speculate. If she hurried, she could go to Mrs. Smead's before supper.

"Mom, could I take a covered dish over to Mrs. Smead? I don't think she eats very well. She might be less confused if she had a better diet."

Ellen dusted off the palms of her hands on her apron. "I've got baked potatoes in the oven. I'll slice off a few pieces of roast and you take it over to her, with some carrot and celery sticks. And fruit—I bet she'd like a fresh fruit cup."

Paige's mother disappeared into the kitchen and Paige clapped her hands together in excitement. Now she could help Mrs. Smead and find out more about this mysterious Sarah Ryan!

———

The old woman seemed clearer today. She'd combed her hair and had the teakettle on the stove when Paige arrived.

"Hello, child. What have you got there?"

"Supper. Baked potato, roast beef, vegetables, and fruit. And I brought three cookies for dessert. Are you hungry?"

"I wasn't, but I am now!" Emma Smead grinned. Her mouth was a collection of yellowed and broken teeth. It should have been repulsive, but Paige liked the shine that a smile brought to the woman's eyes.

As they sat across from one another at the table, Emma began to talk of the past. Paige was thankful that today she seemed lucid and logical, not confused like the other afternoon.

Finally, Paige got around to asking the question she'd come to ask. "Mrs. Smead, who was Sarah Ryan?"

The woman's eyes shuttered and the light behind her eyes dimmed. "Why?"

"Just asking. I heard the name and wondered. I didn't know there was anyone named Sarah Ryan around here."

"There isn't anymore."

"She lived here a long time ago, then?"

"Sarah Ryan doesn't exist anymore." The words were so flat and final that Paige was stunned.

Emma Smead seemed weary after supper. Her head bobbed and her eyes drifted shut. Paige helped her to the bed. Mrs. Smead was asleep before Paige could pull the covers around her shoulders.

Paige gathered the plastic containers in which she'd carried the food. As she turned to leave, Mrs. Smead cried out, "Sarah! The baby! Not the baby!"

Paige spun around and knelt beside the bed. "What baby? Whose baby?"

Emma's eyes flew open and rested on Paige, but the girl knew that the old woman was seeing something far away and long past. "Your baby, Sarah. How could you forget your own baby?"

Paige drew a deep breath. "You mean my baby Michael? My son Michael Bradshaw?"

"No. The older baby." Emma sounded disgusted.

"Lois. You mean Lois."

Emma was getting agitated. "No! The boy! Your first baby boy!"

"But Sarah Cassidy only has two children, Mrs. Smead," Paige said gently. "There was no older boy."

Emma Smead only laughed. "Of course there was! You just don't remember. I remember because I was there when he was born." The old face softened. "What a nice baby he was, too! So fat and healthy." Then her happiness seemed to crumple. "So sad. So sad."

"What was sad, Mrs. Smead? What happened to the baby?"

"I can't tell you that! It's a secret! I promised Sarah to keep her secret!"

Paige swallowed. Her heart pounded like a hammer in

her chest. Her mouth was dry and her lips felt as though they could peel away. She dragged her tongue across her lower lip.

"Maybe I know the secret, Mrs. Smead," Paige guessed. "Maybe it's not a secret to me."

The old woman's vacant stare turned conspiratorial. "You knew about Marshall Ryan, then? And the baby? So sad. So sad." Tears dripped forlornly down the old woman's wrinkle-furrowed cheeks.

Paige couldn't do this to her anymore. No secret was worth the distress this woman was suffering.

"Go to sleep now, Mrs. Smead. Tomorrow we'll talk about Marshall Ryan and the baby boy."

"So sad. So sad . . . ."

The refrain haunted Paige all the way home. Marshall Ryan. A baby boy. Did this have anything to do with Samuel Gardner and the unclaimed inheritance? A foreboding premonition said it did.

The warning message only reinforced the notion.

It wasn't much of a message, really. Only letters clipped from a newspaper and glued onto white typing paper.

STOP THE SEARCH OR YOU WILL SUFFER

It was pasted on Lady Blue's stall. Only Paige entered that stall. It was clearly meant for Paige's eyes alone.

She knew she should be frightened. She knew she should go to her parents with the story. And she knew if she did, she would regret it for the rest of her life.

Something was happening. Something she didn't understand.

Samuel Gardner. Marshall Ryan. A baby boy. Sarah . . . Sarah who?

Surely this was what her mysterious stranger was looking for! Or was it?

Paige chewed her lower lip as she thought. *Who was Samuel Gardner, really? Did he want what he said he wanted? Or were there other reasons for his persuading her to search the farmstead? Had she gone too far? Was this his way of stopping her?* For the first time, Paige felt genuine fear.

With shaking fingers, she saddled Lady Blue. Bryan would know what to do. Bryan would help her.

————

"I don't like it, Paige. I don't like it one bit," Bryan said shaking his head.

He was standing in the sun. A big green John Deere tractor idled at his back. The light danced on his head like flames. But the expression on his face frightened her. He clenched the note in his hands.

"Don't scare me, Bryan," she pleaded.

"You need to be scared. Who would send something like this?"

"I don't know," she admitted.

"Who knows about what you're doing?"

"Just you and Beth and . . . Mr. Gardner."

"I'm afraid he might be dangerous, Paige. I think you'd better tell your parents. Soon."

She looked at him with pleading eyes. She couldn't. Not now. Not when the answers seemed to be getting closer.

"Paige . . ." Bryan's voice was full of warning.

"Bryan, I can't tell my parents now. I'm sure I'm doing the right thing."

"What can be right about getting yourself hurt?"

"Not that. I'm right to solve this mystery for my parents, for my family. It needs to be settled once and for all. I still hear my parents at night, talking, worrying, wondering.

They try to keep it from me, but I know. I know how much it bothers them."

"But—"

Paige rushed on before Bryan could finish. "And I was reading in the Bible—you know, for guidance. I found a passage that tells a story something like mine."

"I know the Bible has lots of answers, Paige, but I'm not sure it covers a set-up like this one." Bryan was half-amused.

"It's in First Samuel—when Abigail stopped David from killing her husband Nabal for not paying his debts!"

"Huh?" Bryan looked baffled.

"David and his men were going to attack Nabal, Abigail's husband, because he didn't pay his debt. Abigail, without telling Nabal, baked a feast and took it to David and his men as a peace offering. She didn't tell Nabal what she was doing because he probably would have stopped her. Instead, she was able to save her husband's life and David's reputation as well. Nabal lived and David wasn't a murderer."

"What does that have to do with you?" Bryan leaned against the purring tractor with a curious expression on his face.

"Don't you see? Abigail's silence wasn't a *deceptive* silence. It was just that she understood her husband Nabal and how he reacted to things. She only had his good at heart—and she saved his life."

"And you have your parents' good at heart, so you have to continue to do what you're doing?"

"Something like that. I don't think we'll ever get over wondering why Grandma put that proviso in the will unless we find the reason. And I'm the only one willing to search for the answer. I can't give up now!"

"Paige, you're quite a girl."

She glanced up at the admiring tone in Bryan's voice.

Her cheeks suddenly felt as red as his hair.

"Then you'll help me?"

"Whoa! I didn't say that!"

"Please?"

"What about Beth?"

"Frankly, I think the less we tell your sister, the better off we'll be."

Bryan chuckled. "You're a hundred percent right. Don't tell her about the note or she'll be checking on plane tickets to China."

"I'm going back to Mrs. Smead's tonight. Can you come with me?"

"What will I tell Beth? I have a date?"

Now Paige felt that embarrassing blush again but she had to quench the wonderful idea.

"You can't. My dad says I can't date till I'm sixteen. That's only a couple more weeks. If Beth thinks you've taken me on a date and blabs, I could be grounded till I'm a hundred and five."

Bryan laughed aloud. "Imagine being grounded for ninety years! I didn't know your dad was so strict."

Paige had to grin at the absurdity. "Maybe we're going to have to take Beth along after all."

"As positive proof that it's not a date?" Bryan was grinning in a heart-stopping, lopsided way. Did he look just a little disappointed?

"Something like that."

"Just don't tell her about the note. She doesn't have to know." Bryan put out his hand and touched Paige's cheek. "You're a brave girl, Paige Bradshaw."

Her legs turned to rubber. Before she could respond, Bryan took the crumpled note from her hands. "I think I'd better keep this at my house. Like you said before . . . just in case."

"Okay." Gathering her wits about her, Paige added, "I

made beef stew. I'll take it over after we finish our own supper. Meet me at the mailbox."

"Deal." Byran nodded. Then, grimly he added, "Paige,
be careful."

She felt a knot tighten in the pit of her stomach as she
nodded. She'd have to be more careful than she'd ever been
in her entire life.

7

*L*ady Blue danced impatiently at the corner as Paige stood high in the stirrups looking for Bryan and Beth. They came riding over the hill, each on a trim quarterhorse. Bryan rode smoothly, as if he were a part of the animal. Beth, on the other hand, was bouncing around on top of her saddle like a rubber ball on concrete.

Paige smiled. Not many people kept horses anymore. The Yorks and the Bradshaws were the only ones who did in this neighborhood. And the way Beth was riding was a sure sign she wasn't going to be a horsewoman, either.

"Yoo hoo!" That was Beth. The "yoo" was loud and clear. The "hoo" came out like a little puff as her lower spine connected with the hard leather of the saddle.

"Hello, there. I thought you were never coming."

"You know Beth," Bryan said by way of explanation. "I couldn't make the stirrups the right length for her. We spent thirty minutes getting her ready to ride."

"Did not! Twenty minutes, tops!" Bryan rolled his eyes at Paige. She covered a grin. She'd been with Beth when she was trying to decide which shoes to wear. Getting her on a horse must have been a monumental task.

"I've never been to Mrs. Smead's," Beth announced. "I've always wondered why that house just doesn't fall down around her head."

"Maybe you'd better stay outside," Bryan offered hopefully. "Just in case it does."

"Is it that rickety?" Beth's mouth puckered.

Paige laughed. "Almost. But I think it will stand through supper."

"Why are we all going to visit her?" Beth wondered aloud. "I don't think I've ever met her."

Bryan and Paige exchanged glances. Slowly, Paige spoke. "We think she may be able to give us some clues as to who Mr. Gardner is."

"You mean she *knows* him?"

"No, but she and my grandmother were childhood friends—sort of like you and me. If my grandmother had wanted to confide in someone, it probably would have been Emma Smead."

"Ooohhh." Beth's perpetual pucker deepened. "I get it!"

The three of them secured their horses and trooped into Mrs. Smead's house.

She was at the kitchen table, knitting. Paige leaned over and spoke loudly into the woman's good ear. "I brought you that beef stew I promised!"

The woman's mouth split in a jagged grin. Beth stifled a gasp. Bryan nudged his sister to silence her.

"You're a good child, Paige Bradshaw. Your grandma would have been proud."

Paige accepted the compliment. She wanted her grandmother to be proud—and her parents, too. She hoped what she was attempting wasn't going to do more harm than good for the family.

Paige decided Emma was looking better as she watched the woman spoon bits of beef and broth into her mouth. She obviously had not been feeding herself properly. Even the little bits of food that Paige had been bringing had given new color to the old woman's cheeks. Paige vowed to come back soon, with more food.

"Delicious!" Mrs. Smead pushed away the empty

bowl. Then her birdlike eye settled on Bryan. "What are you staring at, young man? Am I that old and ugly?"

Bryan nearly swallowed his tongue. "No, Mrs . . . no! I was just, uh, well . . ."

Beth came to the rescue. "He's always staring at people, Mrs. Smead. He tries to imagine what they're thinking or how they used to look when they were young. Weird things like that. That's why he and Paige get along so well. They're always trying to figure things out that no one else even thinks about."

The woman cast a sly glance between Paige and Bryan. "And is that why you're here right now?"

Paige jumped in before she had a chance to change her mind. "Yes. Sort of. Mrs. Smead, you mentioned a woman named Sarah Ryan. Who was she?"

Mrs. Smead's eyes were fixed on the ragged lace of the window shade. "Sarah Ryan was the wife of Marshall Ryan."

"And who was he?"

The old woman sighed. "A drifter, mostly. A handsome drifter. He traveled with the threshing rigs all summer long, harvesting grain, working for a wage."

"Did they ever live around here?"

"Only in Minnesota. Never here. Marshall was older than Sarah. When they married, he was ready to settle down." Emma's hands wove themselves into a knot.

"When was this?" Paige felt an oppressive anxiety falling over her. What if she discovered something she didn't want to know? Her grandmother had spent her girlhood in Minnesota.

A bitter laugh escaped Emma's shriveled lips. "During the Depression. During the poorest, hardest, most miserly part of the Depression."

Paige swallowed. Her grandmother had refused to talk about the Depression or anything that had happened before her marriage to Grandpa Bradshaw. Did this have any bearing on why?

"Did they have any children?"

Emma's face crumpled. "One. One beautiful baby."

Paige could sense that Beth and Bryan were holding their breath. "What was the baby's name?"

Suddenly, without warning, the soft, reminiscing expression in Mrs. Smead's eyes turned wild. It was as though a curtain had been drawn over her memories of the past. "I can't tell you! I can't tell you about the baby! Sarah made me promise! 'The baby died,' she said. That's what I'm supposed to say! 'Don't talk about the baby, Emma.'" Her eyes found Paige's. "You can't ask me about the baby!"

The old woman tried to stand. The wooden chair clattered to the floor. Her balance wavered.

Bryan shot from his own chair and caught her as she fell.

As they helped her to bed, the old woman pleaded, "Don't tell Sarah I told you about the baby. She didn't want anyone to know what they had done. Sarah would never forgive me if I told anyone about the baby . . ."

Beth was huddled in a chair in the corner, her eyes wide as Frisbees.

Bryan turned to Paige, his expression as stern as she'd ever seen. "This woman needs a doctor."

Paige nodded. "I'll go get Mom."

None of the threesome mentioned Mrs. Smead's odd words as they galloped for home. There was no time to speak after the Bradshaws were alerted to Mrs. Smead's condition. It wasn't until the last red flashes from the globe atop the ambulance disappeared, that Paige had a moment alone with Bryan.

"There *was* another baby, Bryan. My grandmother's baby."

"You think Sarah Ryan and Sarah Cassidy are the same person?"

"I'm sure of it. My grandmother had a child before she had Dad and Aunt Lois. That had to be what Mrs. Smead was talking about."

"You don't know for sure."

"Sarah Ryan. Sarah Cassidy. It had to be. My grandmother was married and had a child before Dad and Aunt Lois."

"What happened to her first husband?" Bryan asked logically. "And what happened to the baby?"

A lump the size and consistency of a flour dumpling lodged in her throat. "I don't know. Something awful, I think."

"Now you're beginning to sound like Beth," Bryan joked lamely. He paused for a moment before adding, "This is getting scary, Paige. I don't like it."

"I don't like it either," she admitted. "But what can I do about it?"

He shrugged. "Quit asking questions."

"What about Mr. Gardner?"

"You don't owe him anything, Paige."

"I gave him my promise."

Bryan looked at her with admiration in his eyes. "And you think that's pretty important, don't you?"

Paige nodded. Promises were to keep.

Bryan sighed deeply, his broad chest pressing against the wash-worn chambray of his shirt. "Then I'll still help you. We'll try to get this whole thing settled by the time Gardner returns."

Paige offered him a grateful smile and she carried home with her the gentle squeeze Bryan placed around her shoulders. But even the memory of that tender moment couldn't erase the nagging thought boring at the back of her head.

Bryan had said he would help her solve the mystery before Mr. Gardner returned to Nashton.

But what if Mr. Gardner had never really left?

Paige couldn't get the idea out of her mind.

All day, as she sorted boxes and moved discarded furniture in the attic, she thought about it.

What if Gardner hasn't left as he promised? What if he was the one who put that note in Lady Blue's stall? What if he really doesn't want me to find out what happened to Grandma Bradshaw's first baby?

Paige's head ached with the mystery. If Gardner didn't want the existence of that baby to be discovered, why had he sent her on this search?

Perhaps he didn't think she'd learn anything to disprove that he was a rightful heir. Perhaps it *was* a ploy to claim the inheritance. Perhaps her parents were right after all.

But the sad-faced man kept popping into the middle of her logic and scattering it on the wind. His eyes, so sad and pleading, had been honest. His distress had been real, she was sure.

Confused beyond measure, Paige sat in the middle of the attic floor and prayed for guidance. It would come, she was sure. Now all she had to do was wait.

"Are you done up there, Chapter?" Mike Bradshaw yelled from the second floor. It was nearing suppertime.

"I have to lay out the scatter rugs I have hanging on the line and it's all finished," Paige called back.

The attic gleamed like it had never gleamed before. The windows glittered like diamonds. The newly waxed flooring had a store-bought luster. Every packing box was dusted and organized by size and content.

And there hadn't been a clue in the entire place. Not a hint. Nothing. There was no sign that Sarah Cassidy Ryan Bradshaw had existed before her wedding day in 1939.

Paige sighed. It was a lot of work for little reward, but maybe she'd have more luck in the barn.

The Bradshaw barn was a traditional North Dakota symbol—a red wooden structure with a green-shingled, hip-roof design. Two metal cupolas decorated the ridge of the roof, ventilating the building and giving it a stately, important appearance.

The great door was open, Paige noticed as she peered out the attic window, as if the building were just waiting to be explored. But it would have to wait. Supper was ready.

"Have you heard how Mrs. Smead is?" she asked as she piled mashed potatoes onto her plate.

"Better, last I heard. That poor woman was malnourished. I feel so terrible. I should have been checking on her more closely." Ellen shook her head.

"Good thing Paige was faithful," Mike commented. "At least she got some decent food over to the house."

"Will she be all right?" Paige inquired as she made a hole in her mashed potatoes. Though she didn't do it in front of guests, she still liked her potatoes and gravy to make a little volcano on her plate. Intently, she designed the cone and little ridges for the lava-gravy.

"I hope so. She and Grandma Bradshaw were so close. When Grandma was alive she always looked after Mrs. Smead. I'm afraid we've neglected her badly these past months. She must have been terribly lonely."

"Tell me about Grandma and Mrs. Smead." Paige's question sounded casual.

"They were 'like soup and a sandwich,' your grandmother used to say, 'always better together.' "

"They grew up together?"

"They met as children. Then they both attended a teacher's college in Minneapolis. Mrs. Smead came out here to teach. Grandma came in 1939 to marry your grandfather. And they lived only three miles apart from then on."

Paige finished her meal in thoughtful silence. *So Mrs. Smead did know about those lost years in Sarah Cassidy's life.* But would she recover enough to answer Paige's questions?

Her determination renewed, Paige sauntered into the farmyard. The night was warm and fresh, like North Dakota summer nights usually are. It was still light. On impulse, Paige headed for the barn. She had an idea.

To her left as she entered the barn was the room they called the office. It held extra bridles, reins, and whatever else was needed for the horses. It was little used and musty now. Rows of liniment and ointments lined one wall. There were dusty account books that held the lineage of all the animals that had ever inhabited the Bradshaw farm.

Her father had started a license plate collection on one wall and a sack of feed nearly blocked her way into the room. If there were going to be clues about Sarah Cassidy, she might find them here. Her grandmother had done much of the bookkeeping for her grandfather.

Paige knew she was clutching at straws, but, as she had reminded Bryan, she had promised. She had promised Mr. Gardner a thorough search of the farmstead and she'd give him that. Then he would have to leave.

She forced the question of the baby Mrs. Smead had mentioned into the back of her mind. She either had to prove the baby was Mr. Gardner or prove it wasn't. For herself. For her grandmother. Even for Mrs. Smead.

The cavern of the barn was dark and silent. It was darker in the barn's office than she'd expected. She tripped on a pile of discarded leather straps.

The single lightbulb hanging unshaded from the ceiling cast an eerie glow about the room. Paige sneezed as she thumbed through the dusty books.

Nothing. There was nothing.

Thoughtfully, Paige wandered out of the office. She and her grandmother had come here often to feed the latest batch of kittens. Grandma would warm milk and doctor it with an eyedropper of cod liver oil. Then they would take disposable pie plates of the mixture and climb to the loft.

The mama cat, wary and unwelcoming, would come and taste the peace offering. Soon, if she and Grandma sat still enough, there would be a flurry of skritches and scratches and the kittens would start to peek out of whatever hiding place their mother had found for them.

Paige and her grandma would freeze like statues until the kittens meandered close enough to drink. Paige had learned to move quickly and grab a kitten as it ate. She would scratch behind its ears until she felt it calm down and start purring. Then she would put it down next to the milk again. That kitten would be easier to catch the next time, and the next. Within a week, they would have the whole litter eating from their hands.

She climbed the dusty wooden steps to the loft. A covey of pigeons fluttered in the peak of the barn. Paige gingerly tested the floor as she stepped into the hayloft.

Her father always warned her to beware of the uncovered opening over the feed passages below. He forked hay down the roughed-in holes to the cattle beneath. She could break a leg by misstepping and plummeting through one of the hay chutes.

Paige was edging away from the trap door to the loft when her toe snagged on a rise in the floor. Her arms flailed for balance. As she teetered forward, the floor and the mouth of the hay chutes came toward her.

She heard a scream and, suddenly, realized it was her own. Paige tumbled, head first, through an open hole in the barn floor.

She couldn't inhale. Her breath was knocked out of her as she landed across the wooden divider between the mangers. She saw a smattering of silver stars whiz before her eyes.

The pain was intense. Gulping and gasping for air, Paige clawed her way out of the feed trough. Tears streamed from her eyes.

"Paige? Paige? Are you in here?"

Bryan! It was Bryan!

"Paige!"

He was holding her, rubbing her back. The air was flooding into her burning lungs.

"What happened?"

"I . . . got . . ." the words came in gasps, "the wind knocked . . . out . . . of . . . me."

"Where did you fall from?"

"Up there." She pointed to the hole in the ceiling.

"How'd you do that? You've been up there a million times!" Bryan seemed less frightened now that Paige was catching her breath.

"I dunno. I tripped on something."

His face showed concern. "On what?"

"I don't know. Something."

"Can you walk? I should get you to the house."

Paige nodded weakly. "Stupid stunt. I should have looked where I was going."

"Maybe," was all he would say.

He gently helped her to the farmhouse. Mike and Ellen were settled on the porch and came running when they saw their dirty, straw-covered daughter limping forlornly next to Bryan.

Paige lost track of the boy as her mother insisted that she go inside and take a warm bath, but he was on the porch with her father when she returned from bathing, wrapped in a turquoise robe, her hair damp from washing it.

"Are you all right?"

"Fine. Except for my pride, which was mortally wounded."

Mike grinned and stood up. His rocking chair

swooshed behind him. "I think I'll go inside and leave you two to talk."

Paige shot him a grateful glance. Maybe he'd said she couldn't date yet, but at least he was allowing her to have Bryan as a friend.

"Are you sure you're okay?" Bryan's eyes were unusually dark and troubled.

"Positive. Why so serious? I just tripped and got the wind knocked out of me!"

"Maybe."

His tone alarmed her. "What?"

"I went back into the barn, Paige. Up to where you said you tripped and fell."

"So?"

"I found this." Bryan held up two thick pieces of weathered wood with nails jutting from their surface.

"And what's that supposed to mean?"

"They were nailed to the floor next to the hay chute, under the straw where you tripped."

"Huh?" She gave him a blank stare. She'd never noticed anything like that before. She was frightened by the grim look in Bryan's eyes.

"They were covered with straw so they couldn't be seen. Your toe must have hit one and sent you through the hay chute and down into the manger below."

"I wonder why it was there," Paige mused. "What would Dad have done that for?"

"I don't think your father nailed these boards to the floor, Paige."

"Who then?" she asked, a little impatiently. Bryan was getting as jumpy as Beth.

"I don't know, but the whole floor up there is booby-trapped. Sooner or later, someone—probably you—was bound to go up there and trip on one of these strips."

Suddenly she was frightened. It came over her like a

tidal wave—one moment she was dry and secure, the next, damp and uneasy with fear.

"Bryan?" His name came out in a shallow squeak.

"Somebody wanted to hurt you, Paige. No one goes into the loft in the summer but you. The cattle are grazing. Lady Blue and the kittens are all that's inside the barn most of the time." He paused to let the information sink in. "And you're the only one who takes care of either Lady or the cats."

She shivered in the night air.

"But why?"

"Maybe they want to stop you from doing something."

"What?"

"Looking. Looking for information about your grandmother."

"But only you and Beth and Mr. Gardner know about . . ." her voice trailed away.

"Beth and I don't want to hurt you, Paige."

"But why should Mr. Gardner?" she wailed. "I'm trying to help him!"

"Maybe. Or maybe not. You've got to stop, Paige. No matter what you promised him. Things aren't going like they should."

"I can't stop."

"Mr. Gardner isn't worth it, Paige. He could be the one who wants to hurt you."

"It's not about Mr. Gardner anymore, Bryan."

"What's it about then?"

Bryan looked so worried it made Paige want to weep. But she couldn't stop. Not now. "It's about me. I need to know for my own sake, Bryan. I need to know about my grandmother."

"You know all you need to. You've known her all your life."

"But I don't think I ever understood her! Don't you

see? She must have had things happen to her that I can't even imagine! I want to understand who she was—who she *really* was."

Bryan sighed. "Then I'll have to watch you more closely. You can't be tumbling down holes and nearly breaking your neck in some crazy search for self-discovery."

Paige smiled a wavery but appreciative smile. "You're a good friend, Bryan."

He smiled back. The light from the living room caught the even white line of his teeth. "So are you, Paige. So are you."

Before she knew what was happening, he leaned over and tenderly rumpled her freshly washed hair. Gently, he ran his thumb along the curve of her cheek. By the time Paige recovered from her surprise, Bryan had slipped away into the night.

Giddy—with either happiness or weariness or a combination of the two—Paige stared for a long time into the darkness. Nothing in this sixteenth summer was as she'd expected it to be.

8

"*Evan* called and he's asked to come over." Ellen made her announcement at breakfast.

"Is Lois coming?" Mike wondered aloud.

"No. He wanted to come alone."

"He knows the rules I set up. He can't be here without Lois. The first day Evan is allowed on the farm is your birthday." Mike's jaw was grim and tight.

"It's okay with me, Dad," Paige offered. "Evan should have realized by now that . . ."

"I think it's going to take more than banishment from this farm to teach him a thing or two."

"But he's looked so unhappy!" Paige complained. "He sits at the corner, you know, where his mailbox is, and stares down here like it's a lost treasure!"

"He should have acted better when he was here. Then he would be welcome."

Paige knew her father was right. Evan needed rules and regulations and someone to love him enough to enforce them. Every kid needed that—whether the kid knew it or not.

She hadn't seen Bryan or Beth for days. Bryan was doing the last of the seeding this year. It was the first time his father had trusted him with the drill and had expressed confidence in his son to make the rows symmetrical. With Bryan in the field, Beth got chicken house duty as well as the garden and indoor responsibilities.

But today Beth was coming over. The two girls had planned it on the phone the evening before. They were going to have a picnic. Beth had seemed reluctant at first, Paige noticed; but when Paige assured her friend that Evan would be nowhere in sight, Beth's normal enthusiasm returned.

When Beth arrived, she was lugging a huge woven straw basket.

"What's in there? It looks like enough to feed Minneapolis!" Paige commented. The basket was half the size of Beth.

"Suntan lotion. My radio. A book. Nail file. Polish. Baby oil so I don't shrivel up like a prune . . ."

"Beth, you'll never shrivel up like a prune," Paige announced. "You'll just turn into one gigantic freckle. Anyway, I thought this was a picnic. Where's the food?"

"That's in here too." Beth set the hamper on the ground. "Sliced ham, buns, pickles, hard-boiled eggs, Kool-Aid, a chocolate cake . . ."

"Are you sure there'll be enough for the two of us?" Paige inquired teasingly.

"Bryan said he'd have lunch with us. I *had* to bring lots."

Paige's heart soared, but rapidly plummeted again when Beth commented suspiciously, "I wonder why he's so interested in having lunch with us. He used to think you and I were dumb."

"He did?" Paige tried to keep the disappointment from her voice.

"Sort of. But," and Beth cheered up, "he never thought you were as dumb as the rest of the girls. I guess he thinks you're tolerable."

Tolerable. Well, that's better than nothing, Paige thought.

"Where shall we go on our picnic?" Beth asked brightly.

Paige sighed. "I'd planned to go to the Nelson grove, but Dad said no. He thought we should stay on the farmstead somewhere."

"But that's no fun!" Beth wailed. "That's not even a change of scenery!"

"How about down by the east pasture?" Paige suggested.

Beth's face uncrumpled. "You mean by the old car?"

Paige nodded eagerly. It was a pretty spot with a thick carpet of grass and lush wildflowers. Her father had parked an old Packard on a knoll down there. It was her grandparents' first new car and he'd meant to restore it, but had never found the time. Finally he'd put it in the field, "to age gracefully," he said. What he'd really meant was that he needed the storage place in the shed and the car had to go. Anyway, they could go to the knoll and sit in the shade of the old roadster.

"Sure. Come on."

It was a beautiful day. The air was clean and crisp, the colors of the trees and prairies bright. It was as if the world had just been laundered, especially for them. Even sound seemed to travel farther today.

"I can hear Bryan's tractor," Paige commented.

"And his radio. I suppose he needs it that loud to hear over the roar of the engine." The morning news was drifting across the field from the machinery.

Both girls were puffing by the time they reached the knoll. They had to climb a fence to get out of the cow pasture. Beth had a distasteful expression from dodging suspicious "pies" within the fence's confines.

"Yuk!" she yelped as she dropped to the soft grass. "I'm not sure I can eat at all after walking through that series of land mines that the cows left."

Paige grinned. "Some big, tough, farm girl you are! The pasture's a quarter mile behind us. Forget it."

Beth buried her head in the basket. When she finally reappeared, she was frowning. "I forgot the sheet!"

"What sheet?"

"To spread on the ground. I don't want ants and creepy-crawlies disturbing *my* lunch!"

"Beth York! You're the child who used to put more sand in your mouth than you did in your beach pail every time we played in your sandbox."

"I was just a baby. Two or three years old. Anyway, I got my share then. I don't want any ants on me now."

"How can we have a picnic without ants? It's un-American."

"So pretend we're in Europe. Let's eat in the car."

Paige eyed the old roadster. It was still in good shape. It must have been quite a prize when Grandpa and Grandma Bradshaw bought it. It was the first thing they ever really owned after the Depression years passed. Paige could remember her grandmother patting the hood fondly and saying, "This car reminds me of some wonderful days, Paige. Wonderful days."

Grandma Bradshaw always looked sad when she said things like that. Like the days weren't really so wonderful after all. It was a mystery that Paige had never solved about her grandmother. But now, somehow, she felt like she was coming closer to a solution.

Paige jumped at the grinding sound behind her.

Beth had pulled open the passenger door and was peering inside. "We can sit in the front seat and eat our lunch. Come on, Paige. It will be fine."

"Oh, all right," Paige agreed. "But I don't see what's wrong with sitting on the grass. Somehow this old car gives me the creeps. It's getting rusty and . . ."

"We'll leave the door open. You can sit on the side with the steering wheel, and I'll sit on the passenger side. We'll have the food between us and . . ."

Beth was off and running. Paige followed her orders and climbed into the car. There was no use arguing with Beth in one of these moods. Paige settled herself behind the steering wheel and closed her eyes. The fabric seat was warm and scratchy on her bare legs.

She could feel Beth laying out the food and settling herself on the far side of the big bench seat. Just as Paige thought she was about to doze off, Beth announced, "There! All ready! Doesn't that look nice?"

Indeed it did. Beth and her mother had put together a real banquet.

"Beth?"

"Hmmm?" Beth was busy situating herself on the seat facing Paige, her tiny, sun-freckled legs crisscrossed under her.

"What about Bryan?"

"What about him?"

"I thought he was going to eat lunch with us."

"So?"

"How will he know where to find us?"

"I told him to go to your house and ask your mom where we were."

"But we didn't tell anyone where we were going, Beth," Paige pointed out. "Dad said not to go to the Nelson place and I never mentioned coming here."

"He can just eat at home, then," Beth shrugged. "I don't know why he's taken to following us around anyway. He never used to be interested in us. Unless . . ." Beth gave Paige a sharp, knowing glance.

But before she could reflect on any mysterious romantic reasons for Bryan becoming suddenly interested in their friendship, a harsh grinding noise rent the air.

With a heavy shudder, the aging car door slammed shut.

"What happened?" Beth squeaked.

"The door fell shut."

"How could it? I didn't even touch it!"

Paige felt a tickling nervousness in her stomach. "It doesn't matter. Just open it again."

Beth laid down her ham sandwich and tugged at the door handle.

"It doesn't want to move. I think it's stuck."

"It can't be. We got it open without any trouble." Paige leaned over and pressed against it. Nothing.

"Try your side. Maybe this is broken."

With more calm than she felt, Paige pulled against the handle and pressed her shoulder to the door. It was as solid as the other. Nonchalantly, she tried to roll down a window. The handle spun loosely in her hand.

It was then that she remembered her father's words, "That old car needs more work than I have time to give it. None of the windows work properly. You can't roll them down anymore. A person would suffocate driving down the road on a hot day with no breath of air."

Suffocate. Her father hadn't meant it literally, she knew, but the word echoed in her head like the ringing of a bell. The noon sun was directly above them. She could feel the interior of the old car heating up.

"Try the other windows."

"I am!" Beth wailed. "The handles don't seem to be connected to anything inside the doors. Nothing happens."

"Then let's both try pressing on the door to open it. It can't have slammed that tightly shut all by itself."

All by itself.

Paige bit her lip. That door *couldn't* have slammed tightly closed without some momentum behind it. And there wasn't a breeze blowing.

Paige jumped to her knees and peered out the car window. To the east and south there was nothing but gently rolling waves of grass and a long, empty horizon that seemed to go on forever.

Looking to the north she could see the farm buildings in the distance. Grain bins, mostly. Silver bullets pointed toward the sky. Then, squinting her eyes until the muscles of her face ached, she could see someone rounding the farthest bin.

The person was in a hurry, she could tell. Almost as quickly as she spied it, the figure disappeared into the maze of grain bins and augers and trucks.

She shook her head and blinked. Had she really seen something . . . someone . . . hurrying away? Or was that same overactive imagination that kept her doggedly pursuing her grandmother's history also making her mind play tricks on her? She kept staring but no one appeared.

Perhaps it had been her father . . . or Bonzo. . . or Lady Blue . . . or . . .

"Paige? How are we going to get out of this thing?"

Beth's eyes were wide and serious. Her lower lip looked wobbly, as though if she were a few years younger, she'd already be bawling.

"Push harder, I guess."

The two girls worked at the car doors until they were dripping with sweat. The car was heating up in the noonday sun. Paige felt damp between her shoulder blades. When she wiped her forehead, she discovered a clump of hair stuck to her skin.

"Paige?" Beth's eyes were round and frightened.

If only Beth wouldn't keep looking to her for guidance! Paige didn't feel smart enough or strong enough to be brave for both of them. It could be hours before anyone noticed that they were missing—and hours more before anyone found them.

"At least we have plenty of food to last until my dad comes and lets us out," Paige announced with more optimism than she felt. "I think I'll eat some of it right now."

Beth was holding a sandwich to her lips, chewing, gulping, and sobbing all at once. Paige was afraid she'd choke herself.

Glancing at her wristwatch, Paige was surprised to discover that it was only one o'clock. Her father would just be going into the field for the afternoon. Her mother would probably look across the pasture and wonder where the girls had gone. But she wouldn't worry. Not yet.

"Paige?" Beth looked so white and pale that Paige thought she might faint.

"Yes?"

"Bryan told me about the note you found in the barn." Her voice was very small and weak. "Do you think this has anything to do with Mr. Gardner and your grandmother?"

"Of course not, silly!" Paige blurted. She didn't like the thoughts she'd been having put into words. "Mr. Gardner isn't anywhere near here now!"

Or was he? Was the figure she'd seen the same one that had disturbed her family's tranquility? She didn't know.

Two o'clock. The girls were both panting as the heat increased. The air didn't seem as plentiful as it had been. The car was amazingly tight. As Paige ran her fingers around the seals of the doors, she couldn't find a single crack or cranny that might offer them a breath of freshness or a crevice to pry open.

Beth's face was pink and wet. Tears and sweat beaded on her cheeks and shimmered on her jaw. Paige wiped her forehead with a gentle hand.

"Dad will come looking for us soon. I know he will."

Beth gave her a knowing stare. "No he won't."

"Beth!"

"You know it too, Paige. He's seeding. He's not going to even come into the yard until suppertime. And then it will be almost dark. We'll be in this car all night."

Paige didn't reply. She couldn't. There was nothing to say. Beth was right.

Hot as it was, the two girls found themselves comforted by wrapping their arms around each other. As the minutes ticked by, they reminded themselves of past exploits—the raft they built and sailed on the slough, the burial at sea they gave all their dolls when the raft sank into a black bed of slime, the treehouse they decorated, the fine times they'd had together.

Each time Evan's name cropped up, however, Beth's eyes narrowed and her tiny face grew even more tense. "I don't want to talk about Evan. I won't. I can't stand Evan Bradshaw. Let's think of something else."

Finally, when they'd been silent a long while, Beth inquired, "Have you been praying, Paige?"

"Constantly."

"Do you think it's going to work? The prayer, I mean?"

"God always answers prayer."

"But does He always answer them like we want them to be answered? My mom says that God answers prayer, but sometimes the answer He gives is no."

Paige turned her full gaze to her friend, but instead of responding she gave a sharp cry.

Silhouetted behind Beth's head, peering into the car window, was Bryan!

"Bryan!" she squealed. If she could have gotten through that glass, she would have thrown both arms around his neck and given him the biggest, loudest, noisiest kiss either of them had ever known.

Both girls watched in amazement as he bent to the car door, wedged his hand on the handle and pulled it open. Beth and Paige tumbled into his waiting arms.

"You saved our lives! You saved us!" Beth was screaming. Now she gave full vent to the tears she'd been trying to contain.

Paige, on the other hand, was immediately curious. "How'd you find us?"

"I was hungry. Beth promised me lunch."

"Seriously, Bryan. We've been stuck in there for almost three hours."

His eyes became grim. "Three hours? Are you okay?"

"We are now. Thanks to you."

"Paige," he began, and led her away from Beth. "What happened?"

"Beth didn't want to eat on the grass. She forgot to pack something to sit on, so we decided to eat in the car. A wind must have pushed the car door shut." Paige weighed the idea of telling him about the figure she thought she'd seen.

"There is no wind today."

"Maybe there was a gust. Anyway, the door slammed shut and we couldn't get out."

"Would a wind have wedged this under the door handle? There was no way you could have gotten that door open from the inside."

He held a sturdy stick in his hand. It was about ten inches long and had deep nicks in the bark.

"What?"

"Come on, I'll show you."

As Bryan demonstrated, Paige saw him wedge the scrubby stick beneath the door handle. Simple. Clever. Effective. That silly little stick had made the old car a prison.

Without speaking, Paige rounded the car to the other side. There, jutting from beneath the handle was a similar object holding the door in place.

She felt the color drain from her cheeks. She crumpled onto the ground next to Beth.

"Who's doing this, Bryan?"

"Who?" Beth parroted. "Who's doing what?"

"Someone locked you girls in that car," Bryan stated flatly.

"Why?" Beth screeched.

Bryan and Paige exchanged a long glance.

Together they spoke. "The missing baby."

Beth's eyes were as round as saucers. "But that baby had to have been born *years* ago! That baby would be a grown man or woman by now . . ." her voice faded away. When she spoke again, her voice quivered with emotion. "Do you think this has to do with Mr. Gardner? Do you think *he* . . ."

"I don't know if it's Gardner or not, but *someone* doesn't want Paige snooping around this farm for clues to her grandmother's former life. Someone wants to stop her badly enough to hurt her. First the note, then the traps in the barn, now this."

Paige grabbed Bryan by the arm. "Don't you see! I'm on the right track then! I must be getting close to finding something out! I'll have to keep on . . ."

"No." The single word held as much impact as a torrent.

"Bryan! What are you saying?"

"You can't be on this hunt any longer. You might get hurt. You've got to stop. *Now.*"

"But," she stammered.

"If you don't stop on your own, I'll tell your father what we've been up to and he'll stop you." Bryan's eyes got soft and tender. "I don't want you hurt, Paige. Please?"

He cared! Paige weakened. She didn't owe Mr. Gardner anything—not really. Especially if he were the figure she'd seen rounding the grain bins and running away. Nancy Drew or not, after her afternoon in the old car, Paige was half inclined to believe Bryan was right. Maybe this missing baby should stay missing. At least for now.

"Paige?" his voice broke into her reverie.

"Oh, I suppose. For now, anyway."

"Good!" He smiled. "I don't have enough time to go rescuing you sleuths or following you around. No more wandering away by yourselves and no more hunting. You can meet Gardner at the library in a few days and tell him the deal is off. Completely off. Okay?" He chucked her under the chin with his index finger and captured her dark eyes with his own. "Deal?"

"Deal."

"Are you two getting mushy?"

Beth had been silent and they had both forgotten her presence. The little voice jarred them back to reality.

"Damsels in distress are always supposed to be grateful to their knights in shining armor," Bryan teased.

"Well, Mr. Knight-in-Shining-Blue-Jeans, you can just hop back on your tractor. I'm glad you found us, but I'm certainly not going to get mushy!" Beth announced.

Bryan grinned and moved his finger away from Paige's cheek. Then he dipped into the picnic basket for a sandwich. " 'Save 'em and leave 'em,' that's my motto. I'll see you tomorrow."

Paige nodded.

Bryan turned to her again and waved a warning finger, "And remember, *no more sleuthing.*"

Reluctantly, she nodded. No matter how much she wondered about her grandmother, or wanted to solve the mystery about her estate, it was not worth getting hurt over.

The only good thing to come out of this mess, she mused, was discovering that Bryan York cared about her—even just a little bit. He really, really cared.

"Now what are you up to, Chapter?" Mike Bradshaw inquired. Paige had been like a whirling dervish around the house all week. It was as though she had a storehouse of pent-up energy she didn't know how to expend.

"Do you have any sandpaper in here?" Paige was knee-deep in paint cans and her head was obscured by a shelf of supplies.

"For what?"

"I'm going to refinish that old secretary that's in the attic of the bunkhouse. Mom said it was all right. I'm going to put it in my bedroom."

"And how do you plan to get that monster down those steps?"

"Bryan said he'd come over and help me."

Mike sighed. "Then I'd better hang around to see that you don't send the whole thing crashing through a wall. You kids take on more impossible tasks than any other youngsters I've ever known. I've always been terrified that someday you'd try to build an airplane or do brain surgery." Mike shook his head. "What a crew."

Paige grinned. If he only knew what kind of project they'd just given up! But that was over now. In only three days she was to meet Mr. Gardner at the library. Bryan would come with her to confront him. Whatever secrets Grandma Bradshaw had would remain hidden.

Now all Paige had to do was to keep herself from exploding with curiosity. The refinishing job should help.

Her father and Bryan were both dripping with perspiration by the time they got the cumbersome desk and bookshelf combination out of the bunkhouse.

It was bigger than she had remembered—and in need of more work. The once rich stain had darkened until the desk was almost black with age. She'd be stripping old varnish for two days, at least, for the ornate hand-carvings dipped and curled all over the piece. Paige sighed. Once again, she'd tackled a job that was almost too big for her.

"Do you want me to remove the mirror?" Mike asked

as he ran a hand over the wood. Paige could see that he was fond of the old desk.

Then he chuckled. "You know, Paige, I'm glad you're going to refinish this. It was one of my mother's favorite pieces of furniture. In fact," and he slapped his knee with his cap, "I don't know why it ended up in the bunkhouse at all. She used to use it every day. Then, about ten years ago, during that summer that she got so depressed, she had us move it out of the house. It's been in the bunkhouse ever since."

"Grandma was depressed?"

"For a while. We never did figure out what brought it on. Or what shook her out of it, for that matter. She just had a bad summer. When she started to feel better, she didn't want this old secretary around." Mike shook his head and glanced at Byran. "Let that be a warning to you, young man. The Bradshaw women are for the most part aggravating, unpredictable, and temperamental."

Bryan grinned. "You mean like my sister, Beth?"

Mike's laughter winged across the farmyard. "Yes, son, just like Beth."

"Thanks for the warning, sir. I'll keep it in mind."

"You do that. Paige's birthday is coming up soon, and I don't want the uninitiated asking her for a date and getting themselves into anything they can't handle."

Mortified by what her father and Bryan were so casually discussing in front of her, Paige yelped, "Daddy!"

Two pair of innocent eyes turned on her.

"Oh! You two are just alike!" Paige huffed off to the sound of the two men's laughter. But a spark of pleasure, not dismay, lit her cheeks and her eyes. Almost sixteen. Almost old enough to date.

She already knew who she hoped that first date would be.

9

"*You* really got yourself a project this time, didn't you, honey?" Ellen Bradshaw stood watching Paige scrape curls of chemical muddied with old varnish and wood stain from the drop-door of the desk.

" 'Fraid so." Paige pushed damp hair out of her eyes with the back of her wrist. Her hands were swathed in rubber gloves to protect them from the harsh solvent needed to soften and remove the old varnish.

"Did Dad help you take it apart?" The doors and drawers from the desk lay on a sheet in the shade. The frame, shelves, and mirror were still in one piece and standing in the middle of the yard.

"Just the big door. I did the rest. I've got to take off the mirror before I can strip the varnish from the shelves."

"Anything you want me to tell Mrs. Smead? I'm going into town and plan to stop at the hospital."

Paige glanced up. "Tell her I'll be in to see her soon. And tell her that I miss her."

Ellen smiled. "She'll like to hear that. Poor thing is so alone. I wonder what will happen to her now."

"What do you mean? Won't she get better and come back home?"

"That farmhouse is no place for her to be. There's been some talk of the nursing home, but I don't know if she'd want that."

"I could help her for the rest of the summer," Paige of-

121

fered. "Bring her meals and clean. Stuff like that. Once she's stronger she can do more for herself."

Ellen nodded. "It's a thought. It breaks my heart to see her like this. She and Grandma Bradshaw were so close—if Grandma were alive, she'd be caring for her."

"They really loved each other, didn't they?"

"It was as though they had a special connection that no one else could tap in to. I used to find the two of them deep in conversation every once in a while. It was just like they were keeping secrets from the rest of us." Ellen smiled. "A lot like you and Beth York are today."

"Do you think they had any important secrets?"

"Important? To them, they were. Although I can't imagine what they might have been." Ellen paused. "Emma Smead *did* bring your grandmother through a bad time of depression a few years back. Sometimes I've thought that if it weren't for Emma, we would have lost your grandmother then."

"Daddy talked about that the other day."

"Hmmm. Well, I don't know why, but your grandma spent an entire summer weeping and moping around the house. You were five at the time. You'd climb in her lap and she'd cry even harder. Sometimes I had to send you outside just to keep her calm."

Paige felt a knot building in her belly. "I bothered her?"

"Any child did. The York children upset her as much as you did. But," and Ellen shrugged, "she used to talk to Emma for hours on end. Finally, she seemed to resolve whatever was bothering her and we never heard any more weeping. Pretty soon we all seemed to forget about the incident."

Paige shook her head. She remembered her vow not to do any more sleuthing, but she couldn't stop the questions from forming in her brain. Whatever had bothered her grandmother then seemed tied to the questions Paige had today. But she couldn't think about it. She *wouldn't* think about it. And she'd tell Mr. Gardner so on Saturday.

"There's potato salad and beans in the refrigerator. Slice some cold meat loaf and feed your father at noon," Ellen instructed.

Paige nodded absently, her mind already a million miles away.

Mr. Gardner. Sarah Bradshaw. Sarah Ryan. Emma Smead. The sticks that had held her and Beth prisoner in the old car. The booby-trapped barn. The baby. There had to be a link to all of these jumbled clues. Somehow, some way, they were connected. Who didn't want her to make that connection?

A cold wind gusted from the north. Paige felt a shiver go down her spine. She was scaring herself in a manner that would do Beth proud. She had to stop this nonsense. She'd promised Bryan.

As she scrubbed away at the old desk, she could see Bryan's tractor making wide sweeps in the next field. A smile curved the corners of her lips. Less than a week until she had her father's permission to date. The lips turned down in a frown. What made her think anyone would ask her?

Absently, she rose from her knees and moved to the bookshelves. Until she figured out how to get the mirror off the back of the desk, she was going to have to wait to work on this part. She took a screwdriver and started working at the imbedded metal.

Tiredly, she wiped away a stray strand of hair. Was this doing any good at all? She jiggled the mirror and it seemed to shift. She could hear paper crunching beneath the mirror, next to the back wall of the desk.

Eager to have it done, Paige attacked her project with renewed energy. Finally, the mirror lifted free in her hands. A packet of letters fell to the ground.

Engrossed in getting the mirror to the ground without cracking it, Paige ignored the parcel of papers for a moment. When the mirror was safe, she returned to the yellowed packet of vellum tied in a fine blue ribbon.

She glanced at the address on the envelope.

> Sarah Cassidy Ryan
> General Delivery
> Mankato, Minnesota

Sarah Ryan! It was her grandmother, after all!

Mankato. That was the place that Grandma and Grandpa Bradshaw had met!

With shaking fingers, Paige tore into the packet.

They were letters from Emma Smead. "Emma Grandy" it said on the return address, but Paige knew that Mrs. Smead's name had been Grandy before she married. These were letters from long, long ago.

Feeling like an intruder, but nonetheless compelled to open them, Paige unfolded the pages of the first letter.

January 21, 1929

Sarah,

How very naughty and clever of you to marry that handsome Marshall Ryan! You'll be the envy of all the young women in Mankato when word gets out.

He's much older than you, isn't he? I find that rather exciting. So much more mature, you know. By the way, I know I'm the only person who knows of this event so far. Be sure to tell me when I can start spreading the news!

Which reminds me. I have some news of my own. Do you remember Elroy Smead, that nice young farmer who worked for Mr. Gunderson?

Well, Sarah, he's asked me to marry him! He wants to leave Minnesota and go to North Dakota, since there's some land there he can obtain.

My parents are delighted. I think they were afraid of my being an old maid! Do your parents know of your elopement? My! I wish I could have been a mouse in the corner when that news came out!

Oh, well, you'll have to tell me all about it when next we meet. I'll be home from Minneapolis in a few weeks. I miss you, my dear friend.

All my love to you and that handsome new husband of yours!

With love,
Emma

P.S. Isn't it something how the economy is going? My Elroy says he wishes he had money to invest in the stock market.

Paige felt dizzy with excitement. Proof! Sarah Cassidy *had* married a man named Marshall Ryan. But why had her grandmother kept it a secret? And what had happened to Ryan that freed her to marry Grandpa Bradshaw?

Paige quickly opened the next letter.

It was from Emma again, but nearly three years later than the first.

Dearest Sarah (and Marshall, too),

My Elroy says he's mighty glad now that we were too poor to invest in the stock market. Those men who leapt from windows to their deaths on the first day of the crash had it too easy, to my way of thinking.

They should have had to stay alive and figure out how to make one scrawny chicken feed a family for a week. We've been hungrier than usual, but Elroy says he likes my figure trim. I've heard things are bad for you and Marshall. My mother keeps me posted on your life and times. You know how the ladies are at church—comparing notes on their daughters.

Is it true, Sarah, what I heard? Somehow, through the grapevine, Elroy heard that Marshall had been injured in a fall and lost his job.

If you aren't saying anything to protect your family from worry, I promise not to breathe a word to anyone. If you need help—financial, that is, we really haven't got anything to send.

But (and don't *ever* let on I told you this) I do have the five-dollar gold piece my grandmother gave me. It's been made into a brooch. If Marshall needs medical help and can't afford it, maybe the brooch would speak louder than words.

Do write, Sarah. Tell me if there's anything I can do. You're in my nightly prayers.

> Much love,
> Emma

Paige wiped away the tears on her cheeks. Here was the true story of the Depression. People hungry and poor, eking out a living where there was none to be had. Loving each other more than they loved themselves. How fortunate Grandma Bradshaw had been to have a friend like Emma!

The next letter was dated several months later.

Dearest Sarah—

Hang on! Please! The politicians say this hideous Depression will be over soon. I realize that Marshall has not worked in months, but neither have many others. It's the news of your pregnancy that is distressing you now. Don't despair. There will be money to feed and clothe the child. You and I will make sure of that.

And remember, what a child needs most is love. Your child—yours and Marshall's—will be rich in the most important way of all. If you can give love, the rest won't matter.

> All my love,
> Emma

The baby! This was the baby Mrs. Smead had talked of

*when her mind was wandering! This was the unnamed heir of
her grandmother's will! And Mr. Gardner—was this baby actually Mr. Gardner?*

Paige was trembling so that her teeth chattered. She felt
cold and fluttery inside. A gust of wind scraped a branch
across the picture window of the house, making her stiffen.

She, unbeknownst to anyone else, was peering into the
past—her grandmother's, Mrs. Smead's, her parents', even
her own. She felt guilty, somehow, to have found out about
this personal unhappiness of her grandmother's.

Her elopement with a man called Marshall Ryan. His
injuries, whatever they might have been. A pregnancy when
there was not enough food for the mouths already in existence. The poverty of the Great Depression, the series of
years that made rich men poor and strong men weak. It was
no wonder Sarah Bradshaw had chosen not to speak of her
past.

But what had happened to Marshall and the baby?

There was a single letter left in the tiny packet. This
letter was not in Emma Smead's spidery scrawl. There was
no address and the letter had remained unmailed. Across
the front, in her grandmother's own hand were the words:

To Whom It May Concern

Was it she? Paige wondered. Was she the one who had
a right to be concerned? Was it her right to read the letter?
Her duty? The image of her mother crying and her father
frowning came to her mind.

Paige studied the yellowed envelope. This was the key.
To open it might be the answer to Mr. Gardner's quest. To
open it might be the answer to the question of a missing heir.
To open it might point a finger at whomever did not want
her to have this information.

With shaking fingers, Paige pulled the letter from its
fold. There were muddied spots upon the page, as if the let-

ter had found its way into the rain. Or was it tears?

It was dated September, 1934.

To Whom It May Concern:

I don't know how else to begin this letter, because I do not know your name.

Odd, isn't it? After all, you are my son.

My son. You have no idea how wonderfully sweet those words sound on my lips. *My son.*

I've always dreamed of having a son—a big, strong, strapping boy like Marshall. I wanted for you your father's wisdom, his kindness, his compassion. I wanted a son who would know his father's strength.

But time and circumstances play odd tricks on dreams. And this accursed Depression is playing tricks on all of us.

Your father has been injured. A silly accident, really. But, then, I guess all accidents are silly, hateful occurrences that no one expects or welcomes.

It's worse in a strong man, somehow. When he's suddenly made weak and helpless. Marshall, your father, has prided himself on being a jack-of-all-trades. Now he is master of none.

He was part of a roofing crew that was shingling a church. Marshall was never much for heights. That's why it seems so odd that he was chosen to do the steeple. He must have suffered vertigo and lost his balance.

His back is broken and so is his will.

I've been cooking in a small roadhouse to pay what bills I can. They let us eat free, so neither your father nor I will starve. I've been grateful, too, because healthy food is what a baby needs to grow big and strong.

But, now, the reason for this letter.

Marshall and I have talked, and prayed, and talked some more, about what we should do. He can no longer work. Pale and silent, I see him failing every day. He's not the man I married. My job is perilously close to lost. People need to have money in order to eat. The business may close.

We have nothing.

And we want so much more for you.

It is with a sadness words cannot contain, that your father and I have decided, in order for you, our child, to have a chance at life, you must leave us.

There is a family here who has a lovely farm. Cows. Horses. Other children. Food. And most important, love. They want a little boy.

Tears blurred Paige's eyes until she could not read. She rubbed at her eyes until she saw stars. There was a burning at the back of her throat and she sobbed so that she could hardly breathe. When her vision cleared, she returned her eyes to the page.

So, my child, we are giving you up. Not for ourselves, but for your own sake. To cling to you would be selfish. To give you to a family who can care for you is the largest and the greatest gift we can give.

Your new family wants to extract a promise from your father and me. They want us to vow that we will relinquish all claim to you. I suppose it must be so. If they are to raise you as their own, then their own you must be.

It will not matter for long for your father. He is dying, my child. Dying by inches.

And I will die a little every day of my life. For I will think of you. And pray for you. And wonder who and where you are.

But I will keep my promise. I will never look for you. I have given you the gift of life. It is the first and last gift that I can give to you.

I have made another promise to myself that I will

share with you. I will never mention your existence to another living soul. Oh, my dear friend Emma knows what we have done, but she will never breathe a word. I will go on as though I do not have a knife in my heart, twisting and turning each day.

This is my last communication with you, my child. May it reach you and remind you that you were loved—loved more than you can imagine.

Grow into fine manhood, my child.

Your mother.

Paige was trembling with emotion.

A new vista had opened and she was peering into it with awe. Sacrificial love. Intellectually, she knew what it meant. She'd experienced it in her own personal walk with Christ. And now that gift of Christ's took on new meaning.

As Paige's eyes wandered over the tearstained vellum, another thought sprang to her mind. Mr. Gardner. Was he this child her grandmother had given up?

Paige jumped to her feet. She had to tell someone!

The toes of her tennis shoes stubbed against the grass as she rounded the corner of the house. The car was gone. On the door, her mother had taped a note.

LOIS CALLED. WANTS A RIDE TO TOWN.
DON'T FORGET ABOUT LUNCH.
P.S. DAD IS IN THE WEST FIELD.

Paige couldn't wait for her mother to return. She would go to Lois's right now. Perhaps she could catch them.

The gravel spun out from beneath Paige's feet as she flew toward the barn.

Lady Blue whinnied in surprise at the careless treatment from her mistress. Without a friendly slap on the flanks or her traditional snack from the pockets of her jeans, Paige threw a blanket and light saddle on the filly.

Paige affirmed again and again that the packet of envelopes was tucked into the waistband of her jeans, inside her shirt, next to her skin. Lois would know what to do, Paige assured herself as she galloped toward her aunt's farm. Lois was always level-headed and sensible. She would know how to respond.

Paige scanned the yard for her mother's car. It was empty.

Lady Blue came to a clattering halt in front of the house. Paige threw one leg over the saddle horn and slid to the ground. As she reached the front door it opened.

Evan stood in the darkened portal.

"What do you want?"

"Where's your mother?"

"I dunno. Who cares?"

"I do. And you should."

"Why?"

"Because she's your mother."

"Not my real mother."

Paige bit her lip impatiently. "Yes, she is. She loves you as much as she'd love any other child of hers."

"That's what you think."

"That's what I *know*. Now tell me where she is."

"Your mom came over to pick her up. I think they went into Nashton."

"Okay. Thanks." Paige turned to leave.

"You want to see my new model?" Evan's voice snagged her as she was about to mount Lady Blue. She paused. She was in a terrible hurry. But Even had never made a friendly overture before.

"Sure, why not?" She turned back to Evan and followed him into the house.

This house was similar to her own. They were built within a few years of each other by the same carpenter.

"It's in the dining room," he commented as he led her

through the house. He had the model on a card table in the middle of the room.

It was an airplane, a sleek, fanciful airplane.

"That's nice." Paige commented sincerely.

"Thanks."

"Is that what you've been doing so far this summer?"

Evan turned to her sharply. "What da ya mean by that?"

Her eyes grew wide with surprise. "Nothing. I just haven't seen you much. I wondered if that was all you'd been doing."

"Oh." Suddenly he no longer seemed friendly.

Paige shrugged and turned to leave. She was in a hurry anyway.

"So what have *you* been doing?" His question startled her.

"Cleaning, cooking, things like that."

"Cleaning what?"

Paige gazed at him in surprise. Whatever did he want to know that for? "Why?"

"I was just wondering if you'd . . . found anything that was, well, interesting."

"Interesting how?"

"I don't know. Just interesting."

Suddenly Paige felt strange. What was Evan getting at?

"You'd better tell me what you mean."

"Papers, maybe. Letters, I dunno."

"What would the letters say?"

"Stuff. About that man that's been coming and bothering your mom and dad."

Paige's eyebrow winged upward. "How did you know about that?"

"Lois told me."

"She and Dad agreed not to mention it to anyone. I thought Lois wasn't going to tell you. About Mr. Gardner, that is. They think he's a crook."

"Do you?"

She paused too long before answering.

Evan's eyes took on a sharp, ferrety look. He took a step toward her. "You did find something, didn't you?"

Instinctively, her hand went to the packet at her waist. Evan's eyes followed the quick movement. As she brushed her hand across the band of her jeans, they both heard the crush of paper.

Evan took a step toward her.

The hairs on the back of her neck stood up.

Something was wrong. Very wrong.

10

"*G*ive it here." Evan's voice was harsh.

"Give what here?" Paige challenged, pretending to be brave.

"Whatever you've got. You've found something, haven't you?" His eyes had an odd, predatory look, like a cat stalking a mouse. Narrowed. Intense.

"I don't know what you're talking about," she stalled, backing toward the dining room door. Had they left the screen door open? She couldn't remember.

"Sure you do. Don't play dumb with me, Paige Bradshaw. I heard your dad and Lois talking."

"People talk about a lot of things that are none of your business, Evan."

His eyes took on a glinty, metallic look. "This *is* my business, Paige."

She was surprised at his fervency. Why would it matter to Evan if Grandma Bradshaw had another child?

"Anyway," he continued haughtily, "Beth told me you were hunting for something."

"Beth?" she breathed. "Beth told you that?"

"Oh, don't look so surprised. That little coward runs off at the mouth all the time."

"Coward?" Paige said, watching Evan's face. His lips turned down in a sneer.

"Yeah, a coward. She told me you were looking for some clue that Grandma Bradshaw had another child. She wouldn't have made that up."

"How did you make her tell you, Evan?" Paige spoke so softly the boy had to lean forward to hear.

"Make her? Who says I made her?"

"She wouldn't have told you anything unless she was scared." Paige thought of the venom Beth felt toward Evan. It was not without reason after all.

"She's scared of her own shadow!" Evan scoffed. "I just told her if she wanted to keep Blackie around she'd better tell me what you guys were up to. What an airhead she is!"

Paige's lips tightened into a narrow line. Beth's attachment to the puppy was as strong as Paige's to Bonzo. If Evan threatened to hurt the dog, no wonder Beth had spilled the beans. Evan was one person who seemed able to carry out his threats.

"What did she tell you?"

"She said you promised to look for clues to prove that Lois and Mike have a brother or sister."

"If I said that, what does it matter? It's my home. I can look for anything I want." Her jaw came out stubbornly. She didn't like the way Evan had her trapped against the dining room wall. She was angled away from the door. It would be difficult to escape before he could grab her arm. She eyed the door silently.

"You ain't goin' nowhere. I want to know what you found."

"What do you care?"

Much to Paige's surprise, Evan faltered. The steely look that glazed his eyes flickered for a moment. It shocked her to see, behind the hostile stare, another emotion. Fear.

"I just care. That's all."

He really did. He really cared what she had found. But why?

"If you tell me why you want to know, I'll tell you what I've found. Not before," Paige braved.

"No!" It was more than a command. It was an embodiment of terror. With a lunge so swift that Paige had no time to protect herself, Evan brushed his hand across the card table that held his airplane model.

Paige saw the blades of the scissors even as she saw the look of stark fear in the boy's eyes.

She closed her eyes and screamed.

The shriek echoed in her brain, growing in volume until it sounded like a hundred voices were reverberating in her skull.

Not a hundred voices, she suddenly realized, but three.

Three voices were screaming "no" across the space of the dining room. Her own. And Bryan's. And Beth's.

"Drop it." Bryan had a white-knuckled grip on Evan's wrists. He twisted the hand holding the scissors as he spoke. "Drop it."

Evan whimpered. The scissors clattered to the floor.

Paige's legs felt like rubber. Leaning against the wall, she slid to the floor. Beth was immediately next to her.

"Are you all right? Did he hurt you? Should we call the police?" There was a rim of white etching the perimeter of Beth's lips. She appeared more frightened than Paige.

"The police?" Paige mouthed.

"He tried to kill you. We saw it." Beth turned angry, accusing eyes on Evan.

"I did not!" the boy screamed. Then, as suddenly as he had become incensed, he crumpled to the dining room floor in a boneless heap. "I didn't. I just wanted to scare her. I wanted her to tell me what she found." He turned teary eyes on his cousin. "I wouldn't have hurt you, Paige. I just couldn't lose everything now." He rubbed his eyes with his fists, even though Bryan still had a blood-stopping grip on his wrists. "I couldn't lose it now."

Beth, Bryan, and Paige stared blankly at one another. Whatever was he talking about?

Paige scuttled on her hands and knees over to Evan. Bryan cautiously loosened his grip and kicked the scissors out of Evan's reach. Still, he loomed large over the boy in case he might try to escape.

"Evan?" Paige put her face close to her cousin's. "What do you mean?"

The boy stared at her in disbelief. His mouth worked, but no sound came. Finally, in a tinny, far away voice he asked, "Don't you know?"

Paige put her hands over his and willed him to look into her eyes. "No. I don't. You'll have to tell me. You'll have to tell all of us."

Paige glanced at Bryan over Evan's head. He was pale, tense. He mouthed the words, "Should I call your parents?"

Almost imperceptibly, she shook her head. Evan seemed ready to talk. He'd back like a turtle into his shell if the grown-ups came around.

"Evan? Are you going to tell us?"

Bryan nudged the boy in the back with the toe of his work boot. That seemed to set him in motion.

"You aren't afraid. You don't have anything to lose!" His voice was little more than a pitiful whine.

Not knowing what Evan was so afraid of, Paige leaned closer.

"Afraid of what?"

"Of what you found. Of what it probably says. Of what's going to happen!" Evan's words tumbled over each other in a rush. It was as though he couldn't fathom the idea that Paige was not comprehending his fear.

"You're going to have to explain it better than that, Evan. I don't know what you mean!"

"That's 'cause you're really Uncle Mike's! That's why you're not afraid!"

"Of course I'm Mike's!" Paige chided. "He's my fath . . . father."

The proverbial light bulb went on in her brain. She added, "And you don't think you belong to Aunt Lois, that you aren't her child?"

"I'm not. You know it. I know it. Everybody does. I'm not family. I just live here!" There was a cry in his voice that tore into Paige's heart.

"You *are* family! Every bit as much as me! You just came to us later, that's all!"

"No I'm not. You were born a Bradshaw." Evan shook his head stubbornly. "I'm just a stray Aunt Lois picked up. Like the dogs she gets from the pound or the bottle lambs that no one else wants."

"But Aunt Lois doesn't care where people or animals come from. She loves them anyway," Paige persisted. From the corner of her eye she noticed that Beth and Bryan had both sat down on the floor near her, straining to hear Evan's every word.

Evan's eyes took on a sly, angry look, but he didn't speak.

It was Bryan who spoke up. "I think you'd better explain yourself, Evan. So far you haven't made a whole lot of sense."

Paige leaned back on her heels. She was getting stiff and sore and the tension was gnawing at her. "I think I'm beginning to understand. You didn't want me to find any clues that might lead Aunt Lois or my father to think that they had an older brother, did you?"

Evan hung his head. "It wouldn't have mattered to you. It wouldn't have made a difference to you."

"And what kind of big difference could it have made to you, Evan? What would it matter if there *were* another Bradshaw?" Paige puzzled.

"Don't you see?" His voice pitched to a wail. *"The money!"*

"The money?" All three echoed. "What money?"

"The one-third inheritance Grandma Bradshaw left!" Evan's eyes were wide and pleading. He stared at Paige. "Lois told me that if that money wasn't claimed by the time we went to college, it would be divided between you and me! It would be *ours*."

"But," Paige protested, "if we didn't have that money, then I'm sure our families would help us with college. It doesn't matter, Evan. We can always depend on our moms and dads to . . ."

Suddenly it was terrifyingly clear. Evan didn't believe for one moment that he *could* depend on Lois. Or anyone. Paige's heart twisted.

"You don't believe that, do you?"

Evan shook his head. The lank brown hair fell into his eyes and he didn't scrape it back in that irritating way of his. Paige almost missed the motion.

"Well, I do."

He glanced up. Mirrored in his eyes was the pain of ten years of disappointment. "No one's ever kept me this long except Lois. And she won't keep me much longer. Not once she finds out what I've done."

"Aunt Lois is the one to decide that."

"Evan," Bryan began. Paige and Evan jumped. They'd almost forgotten he and Beth were in the room. "Did you put those booby traps in the hayloft?"

The boy's shoulders sagged deeply.

"Did you?"

"I thought it might scare her off. I didn't want her looking when I wasn't around." A flash of anger bolted across Evan's face. "Uncle Mike said I couldn't come over for a month without Lois along and I didn't want Paige to find anything. I wanted to find it first."

Paige's eyes widened. So, if it hadn't been for that incident with Lady Blue, Evan might have gotten to the information before her!

"And you locked Paige and me in the old car!" Beth accused, her eyes snapping furiously. She puckered up as though she were about to cry. "I thought we were going to suffocate in that old car! You could have killed us! We might have died in that dirty, stuffy old trap!"

Evan squared his sagging shoulders a bit. "No! I would've let you out! I just didn't want you looking anymore! I didn't want you to find anything!" He turned anguished eyes on Paige. "Don't you see? If Grandma Bradshaw had another child . . . and he has children of his own . . . the family would have been bigger . . ." his voice trailed away until the three had to lean forward to hear him, ". . . and no one would want me anymore."

There was the heart of the problem. Bryan, Beth, and Paige exchanged glances.

"No one would want me anymore." His voice trailed away in a whimper. Where had the steely-eyed, tough boy gone?

Paige thought she saw a tear shining in the corner of Bryan's eye as he turned his head away. Tenderhearted, quick-to-forgive Beth was loudly snuffling. She jumped up to get a tissue.

"Is that how you really think this family works, Evan?" Paige asked softly. "Really?"

He looked momentarily defiant, then beaten. "It's how the other families I've been in worked. What's so different about this one?"

"What do you mean?"

Evan crossed his legs, leaned his elbows on his knees, and began to talk.

"I can't remember the first home I was in 'cause I was just a baby." As an aside, he added to Bryan, "My parents didn't give me up for adoption, but they didn't want me either, so I couldn't get a permanent family."

Bryan shifted uncomfortably, but continued to listen.

Evan went on.

"I lived with some people called Mr. and Mrs. Rodale next." Evan's eyes took on a faraway look. "They were nice. She made cookies with M&M faces on them. I'd eat the M&M's first, then the cookie." He paused, "Then they had to move. I couldn't go with them, they said, 'cause I was 'unadoptable' and had to stay in the state." Evan's voice choked. "I cried. We all cried."

Bryan's own voice was suspiciously low when he asked, "What happened next?"

"I went to live with some people named Simmons, but I didn't stay there long."

"Why?" Beth poked her nose back into the circle.

"They told the social worker I was a 'behavior problem.' "

"Were you?" she wondered.

"I dunno. Maybe. I didn't want to be with them. I wanted to be with the Rodales. Anyway, the Simmons told the social worker they didn't want me anymore."

"They just gave you away?" Beth squeaked.

Evan nodded. Paige bit her lip. No wonder he felt insecure.

"So what happened next?"

"I lived with Mr. and Mrs. Ridgeworth next." He paused, a tentative smile coming to his lips, then vanishing like a mist.

"Were they nice?" Beth was getting deeply engrossed in this story.

"Yeah. Real nice."

"Why didn't you stay with them?"

"I thought I would, but . . ." and he choked.

"But what?" Beth persisted.

"But they had their own baby and then they didn't want me anymore, either."

Paige closed her eyes. Her head was beginning to ache.

Evan's voice droned on. It was as though he'd detached himself from the rest of the story, as though he were discussing a stranger.

"They said they didn't want a big rough boy like me around their baby. I was seven and I didn't mean to be rough. I wouldn't have hurt their baby if they'd let me stay . . ."

The room was silent.

Evan continued. "Then I lived with Mr. and Mrs. Wilter. They had a whole bunch of adopted kids so they said one more wouldn't hurt. But, then, she found out she was going to have a baby of her own, too. Since I was the only foster kid in the whole bunch, they said I'd have to go." Evan chewed at his bottom lip. "Then the social worker, or somebody, found my real parents and told them they'd better release me for adoption before I got too old and no one wanted me." He paused, a half smile on his lips. "They didn't realize that nobody wanted me already."

"And that's when you met Aunt Lois?"

Evan nodded. "She said she'd like a ten-year-old boy, but I didn't believe her."

"Why?" Beth gasped.

Evan's eyes looked older than his years. "It was a lie. It had to be. No one's ever wanted me."

Paige's mouth felt dry as a straw pile. She'd never dreamed what was going on inside this young cousin of hers. "Is that why you won't call Aunt Lois 'Mother'?"

Evan looked almost angry. "I called Mrs. Rodale Mother. And some of the others. It didn't help."

"You don't understand our family very well, do you, Evan? Not even after five years."

"What are you talking about?"

"My dad and I discussed it when you first came to live with Lois. I asked him how come she wanted an older child, like you, instead of a tiny baby."

"Yeah?" Evan looked interested.

"He said our family worked a little like God's family. We'd love whoever came to us—no matter how old or young, strong or weak, plain or pretty."

"You mean you aren't mad at me?" Evan whispered unbelievingly.

"You bet I'm mad," Paige retorted. "Furious! You pulled the absolute dumbest set of stunts I've ever heard of! You could have hurt Beth and me—badly."

"I thought you said you loved me."

"I do. That doesn't mean I can't be mad at you when you do mean things."

Evan's forehead furrowed deeply in confusion. "I think I'm getting mixed up."

Paige jumped to her feet. "Well, Dad and Aunt Lois can help you figure it out."

She stuck out a hand to help him, but Evan cowered back. "You're going to tell them?"

"No."

"No?" He murmured hopefully.

"*You* are. Right now. Come on."

———

It was a motley crew that found its way to the Bradshaw farmyard. Paige had a determined thrust to her chin. Beth and Bryan were quiet. Evan looked as white as a sheet.

Paige's parents and Aunt Lois were drinking lemonade on the porch.

"Hello, kids. What have you been up to?"

The four of them glanced around. Mike Bradshaw sat up straighter. "Is something wrong?"

Paige smiled. "Not anymore. For the first time in a long while, I don't think there's anything wrong."

"Well, I'd like to hear about that!" Lois laughed.

Paige patted the packet of letters in her waistband and

then she placed her hand in the small of Evan's back and gave him a gentle shove toward the porch.

————

At supper that night, Paige trailed her fork absently through her food.

"You all right, Chapter?" Her father asked.

"Fine. Just thinking."

"Lots to think about, after today."

"What's going to happen to Evan?"

"I don't know. That's up to Lois."

"She won't give him away again, will she?"

Mike smiled. "No. I *am* sure of that. Evan's been tossed around enough for four lifetimes. No matter what happens, Lois won't do that."

"Good. That's what I told him."

"What else did you tell him?"

She shrugged. "Just that we operated kind of like God's family—He loves us in spite of ourselves and we love Evan in spite of himself."

Mike and Ellen laughed aloud.

"I can't think of a better analogy than that, Chapter. And now we know how important it is to show our love to Evan. We thought we were doing it, but it just wasn't quite visible enough."

"Daddy?"

"Hmmm?"

"What about Mr. Gardner?"

"What about him?"

"I promised I'd meet him and tell him if I found anything."

"I think I'll meet him instead, Paige. We have some things to discuss."

"Do you really think he's the one—your half brother, I mean?"

Mike stretched in his chair. "I don't know, yet. But now I'll find out." He laid a hand over his daughter's. "It's quite a shock for me, you know, to find that my mother had kept a secret like this for all these years."

"Was she wrong to do it?"

"Well, it's not what I would have done, but that doesn't make it wrong. She made a promise and she kept it. But after a while, it apparently became so difficult that she was forced to do something about it."

"What do you mean?"

Mike sighed. "Your mom and I have been putting two and two together. The date on that addendum to Grandma's will was ten years ago. August. It was that summer when Grandma was so ill and depressed. I suppose adding that proviso to her will was the one thing she could do for her child without divulging her secret." He paused, and murmured softly, "That, and the letter she never mailed."

"Mom said that at the end of the summer she seemed to get better and it never happened again," Paige volunteered. Mike nodded. "I suppose Grandma felt she'd done what she could. If her first child ever went looking for her, he'd find an inheritance waiting for him. Some visible, tangible proof of her love."

"And what about Samuel Gardner?"

"We'll do some research about him, too."

"Maybe Mrs. Smead could help us," Ellen suggested. "She's supposed to get out of the hospital on Saturday."

Saturday! Paige had almost forgotten! Saturday was her birthday! Then she sighed. That was also the day that her father was to meet Mr. Gardner at the library. The whole family would be in a tizzy by noon, no matter what Gardner said.

No one was even going to *remember* her sixteenth birthday. . . .

11

I was right, no one remembered!

Paige stared glumly into the watery blue remains of the milk on her breakfast cereal. Her mother hadn't offered to fry eggs or make pancakes this morning. She'd appeared so busy that she hadn't even taken time to sit down and ask how Paige had slept.

"Are you done yet, Paige? I want to get those dishes washed up."

Paige pushed her bowl away. "Yeah, I guess. Can I help you?"

"That's all right, dear. I'm almost done. I've got such a mess in the pantry I'd rather be alone. I'm making potato salad."

Paige loved potato salad. She would have been glad to help, but her mother seemed sure she wanted to be alone, so Paige wandered aimlessly out of the kitchen.

She'd slept late. It was nearly eleven. It had taken her a long time to get downstairs for breakfast. She'd showered and blow-dried her hair until it cascaded in a brown wave across her back. No ponytail for her today. Today she was sixteen. All grown up. Almost.

Paige had even spent some time primping before the bathroom mirror. A swish of eyeshadow. A hint of mascara. A dusting of blush. She looked rather nice, even if she did say so herself. Paige studied her reflection in the floor-length mirror in the hallway. She *had* to say so herself! No one was saying it for her. . . .

"Mom?"

"Yes, dear?" Ellen answered absently.

"I think I'll take Lady Blue out for a ride."

"Good idea. See you later."

Paige stubbed her toes in the dirt all the way to the barn. It was this Mr. Gardner mystery. That's why no one had remembered. Mike Bradshaw was in town with Gardner—meeting at the library—doing what *she* should have done!

Even Bonzo was asleep in the sun and didn't want to play. Phooey! What a birthday!

Paige saddled Lady Blue. The dainty filly arched her neck in pleasure as Paige rubbed behind the horse's ear. At least someone was glad to see her!

It was a beautiful day. The colors of the earth and sky were as clear and pristine as an artist's freshly prepared palette.

Paige gave Lady Blue a nudge and the little filly trotted toward Mrs. Smead's ramshackled house. Perhaps Lady thought she was going to spend another day tied to the wire of the old clothesline in the yard. Paige had spent the better part of the prior afternoon cleaning and scrubbing the house. It was ready for Mrs. Smead's return.

Ellen and Mike had filled the cupboards with groceries—tea, sugar, instant coffee, potatoes, canned meats and vegetables—simple things that either Paige or Mrs. Smead could prepare. Paige would spend two or three hours a day with the old woman for the rest of the summer. That way Mrs. Smead would have time to decide for herself where she would like to live in the fall.

Tugging Lady Blue's reins to the right, she turned toward the Yorks'. Maybe Beth had remembered what day it was.

But she had no luck at the York home either. The garage was empty and no one answered the door.

Paige sighed. She could go to her Aunt Lois's, she supposed, but she felt a bit like an intruder there. Evan had seen a counselor, and Lois was spending every free moment with him, trying to untangle the web of insecurity with which he was burdened.

Already, Paige could tell that Evan was feeling better about himself. She'd heard him call Aunt Lois "Mom." She'd watched his eyes roam to Lois's face and had seen the relief that sprang to them when Lois had naturally and unquestioningly responded.

It was difficult to forget what Evan had done, but, already, the frightening circumstances seemed to be fading from her memory. Paige was glad. She only wanted to remember the best about her cousin.

An embarrassing growl came from her mid-section. Three gurgles followed. Paige glance at her watch.

Four P.M.! She'd missed lunch!

Nudging Lady Blue's round sides with her heels, she sped for home. As she neared the farmstead, she noticed the cars in the driveway. The Yorks' big blue stationwagon. Aunt Lois's van. Her father's pickup. And, could it be? The battered old Chevy that had coasted into this yard four weeks ago?

She gave Lady Blue a whomp in the sides that sent the horse galloping.

"Here she is!" Her father hollered as she slid from Lady Blue's back. "I thought we were going to have to have this party without her!"

Party? Paige blinked. On the porch sat Lois and Evan, Mr. and Mrs. York, Beth and Bryan, Mrs. Smead, and . . . most amazing of all, Mr. Gardner.

Before she could speak, the group broke into song. "Happy birthday to you! Happy birthday to you! Happy birthday, dear Paige . . ."

Bonzo and Blackie started to yip in chorus. The slightly

off-key group faltered. The song finished in a flurry of chuckles.

"Well, are you surprised?" Beth demanded to know.

"That's putting it mildly," Paige acknowledged. "I thought everyone forgot."

"Forgot!" Mike whooped. "Chapter, you underestimated us!"

Paige looked sheepish. After the events of the last month, that's one thing she shouldn't do—underestimate the caring of her family.

Before she could say anything, Mr. Gardner unfolded himself from his chair and came toward her.

"Hello, Paige."

"Hello, sir."

"I hear I have much to thank you for."

Her eyes widened. "Then you *are* . . . I mean, the letters . . . the will . . ."

"Yes," he laughed. The corners of his eyes crinkled in very nice smile lines.

That was what was different about him! He didn't look sad! In fact, he looked rather delighted.

"I'm Samuel Ryan Gardner, your uncle."

"Really? I mean, for sure?"

The smile lines deepened. "For sure. Your father and I had some documents verified today. And," he turned to Mrs. Smead in the big green rocker, "Emma provided the clinching evidence. She recognized this." He pulled up his shirt-sleeve to reveal a small strawberry birthmark on his arm.

"Sarah Ryan's baby had a strawberry birthmark in this very place. I don't think we can get more certain than that."

Paige's eyes traveled from the mark on Gardner's forearm to Mrs. Smead. She looked wonderful. Her hair was combed into a soft bun at the nape of her neck. She wore a lavender dress with a high, frilly collar. At the neck was a brooch. A five-dollar gold piece.

The old woman's eyes were clear and her voice lucid as she announced, "This is the happiest day of my life. To think," and her eyes traveled from Gardner to Paige and back again, "I'm seeing Sarah's children united."

Her hands twisted in her lap before she continued. "I didn't think it would ever happen, you know. Not after Sarah made that promise not to look for her baby or mention him again. And not after Marshall died."

"What happened to him, Mrs. Smead?"

Emma sighed. "He just sort of withered away after the accident. One infection followed another. One night he fell asleep and didn't wake up." She sighed again. "I think it broke his heart to see Sarah suffer and know it was because of him they didn't have food or money to keep the baby."

Mrs. Smead's eyes lighted on Gardner. "They loved you, you know. More than words can say."

Gardner nodded. "I realize that now." He sat down on the top step of the porch and stretched his long legs out before him. "And that's the most important part of this search of mine, finding out the reasons." He gave a shadow of a smile. "I was always afraid that I'd find out I was an unwanted child, but I had to know. To learn that I was loved so much . . . well, I can't tell you what it means."

His eyes traveled to Evan. "I believe you can understand that, son."

Evan raised his head. Paige had never seen so much peace in his eyes. "Yes, sir. I can." Then he continued, his young voice shaky. "And I'm sorry I didn't want Paige to help you. I thought, well, I thought . . ." His voice trailed away.

"I know. Your Uncle Mike told me." Gardner stretched. It was still difficult for Paige to imagine that he was her uncle, but she liked the thought. "I've been thinking about all this, and perhaps there's something I can do to set everyone's mind at rest."

All eyes settled on Samuel.

"I know one-third of Sarah Ryan Bradshaw's estate is waiting for me. I understand that she and Emma Smead concocted that idea to keep my mother from going mad with the thought that she'd given up her child. But," and the beagle-like face lit with pleasure, "even though you can't tell it by the condition of my car, I'm not an impoverished man."

Paige and all the other listeners leaned forward to hear what was coming next.

"I have two children of my own. Twins. They'll be starting college this fall. As I've talked with you, I realize what my mother would have wanted for her legacy. With your permission, I'd like to divide my portion of the inheritance five ways and give each of Sarah Cassidy Ryan Bradshaw's grandchildren enough money to pay their college tuitions. There's plenty of money and accrued interest to do just that. Don't you think she would have liked that?"

Ellen was mopping her eyes and Lois was openly crying. Evan stared at Gardner as though he'd just landed in a spacecraft. It was Beth who finally spoke.

"But you said *five* ways! There are only *four* grandchildren!"

Samuel smiled. "That's right. I thought, if no one had any objections, I could give the remaining fifth of the inheritance to Emma Smead. I have a feeling my mother would have wanted it that way."

Now *no one* had dry eyes. Even Bryan and Mr. York looked suspiciously uncomfortable and they turned their heads away. Emma dabbed at the corner of her eyes with a fragile lace handkerchief.

Paige jumped up and grabbed him by the hands. "That's the nicest thing I've ever heard!"

Gardner smiled. "And being welcomed into this family is the nicest thing that's ever happened to me."

"But how'd you find out about the Bradshaws?" Beth asked, curious as ever.

Gardner tipped his head toward the red-haired girl. "My parents—my adoptive ones, that is. I always suspected that there was something different about me. I'm big and lanky. They're both small-boned and frail. I have a bunch of red-haired sisters like you and I'm certainly no redhead. For years my parents had kept from me that I was adopted. When I found out for sure I was adopted and started to search for my real parents, they didn't tell me that they knew. I hunted for many years without knowing they had that information."

Gardner's eyes darkened with sadness. "It wasn't till both of them were ill and not sure they'd be alive much longer that they admitted my parents' names were Sarah and Marshall Ryan." He shrugged. "I just took that bit of information and went from there."

"And you landed in our yard," Paige finished.

"And you almost got us killed," Beth accused dramatically. Evan looked like he wanted to shrivel up and blow away.

"I'm sorry about that," Gardner announced.

"So am I." Evan's voice was small but sincere. Even Beth had the grace to look forgiving.

"Dreams come true, 'deed they do. 'Deed they do."

All heads swiveled toward the rocker. Emma Smead moved to and fro in the big cane chair. " 'Deed they do . . . 'deed they do."

A tear sparkled in the corner of one eye. Her workworn hands knit together, the backs looking for all the world like road maps. " 'Deed they do."

"Emma, are you all right?" Ellen worried.

"Me? I'm as fine as I can remember being in years,

thanks to all of you." Emma smiled. "It's a dream come true, you know, for me to see Sarah's son again. He looks good and healthy now. Like he was fed and loved for the better part of his life."

Then she looked Samuel Gardner right in the eye. "That's what she wanted for you, you know. To be fed and loved. She would have kept you if she could have fed you, 'cause no woman ever had more love to give."

"I know that now." Gardner's voice was husky with emotion. Paige felt her lip quiver.

"I would have told Mike and Lois about you myself if I hadn't made the vow to Sarah." Emma shook her head. "I should never have made that promise, but after Marshall died, she had no one but me. Then when she met Mr. Bradshaw, she was so happy, so carefree, that for a few years it didn't seem to matter. She seemed to forget her past. It wasn't until," Emma spit out the words that seemed distasteful to her, "*that summer*, when all the memories came flooding back."

"The year that Mom became so depressed?" Mike concurred.

"Aye, that's the one. That's when we came up with the plan." Emma's head bobbed.

As Emma spoke, Bryan moved behind Paige and took her hand.

Emma continued. "The plan to add a clause to her will. Sarah had been thinking about the baby she gave up. She couldn't seem to quit thinking about him. But she'd promised never to try and contact him. She was beside herself with wanting to do something for her firstborn."

Emma's eyes focused somewhere in the sky and on the past. "I'd suggested that she put something in her will. That way, she wouldn't be breaking her promise to the family to try and reach the boy. Once she was gone, it shouldn't matter."

Mrs. Smead smiled. "Sarah liked that idea. It made her feel like she was doing something, not just dwelling on what could have been. But," and Emma frowned, "we didn't know much about the boy—his name, or where he lived. Sarah knew the family had moved to ensure the adoption was kept secret. That was why the addition was so sketchy. But," she brightened, "we decided to do it and then pray that if the Lord so willed it, the boy would find his way here."

She rested her pale, aged eyes on Gardner. "Dreams and prayers do come true. 'Deed they do."

Everyone was silent, considering Emma's awesome story.

Ellen slapped her hands on her thighs. "My emotions can't take any more. I'm either going to have to go in the house for a fresh handkerchief or we're going to have to give Paige her birthday presents!"

A cheer rose from the younger section of the group, especially Beth.

"Open mine first, Paige!" Beth begged. "You're gonna love it!" She thrust a thick package into Paige's hands.

"What is this? A dictionary?"

"Open it! Open it!" Beth was wiggling on the step like Bonzo sitting on an anthill.

Paige peeled away the paper. Inside was a scrapbook with words stenciled on the front.

THE MYSTERIOUS SUMMER
BY BETH YORK

"I wrote a book about our adventure, Paige! A mystery! Don'tcha love it?" Beth took the thick book from Paige's hands. "Here's where we search the attic." Her fingers danced across the pages. "And here's where that humongous bird attacks us. And this is the place where the hundreds of bats swoop down on us. Oh, yeah! And here's where we're locked into an airtight room by an evil scientist. . . ."

"Whoa!" Paige laughed. "I thought this was about what happened to us this summer!"

"It is—sort of. But nothing was really *that* scary, so I kind of . . . elaborated . . . a little."

"If I remember correctly, you were pretty scared at the time," Bryan commented.

"I was not." Beth stuck out her tongue.

"Were too."

"Was not."

"Okay, you two. We get the picture," Mr. York broke in. It was obvious that he hoped to retire soon as referee of these sparring matches. "Open some more presents, Paige."

There were clothes from her parents, an antique fan from Mrs. Smead, a vial of perfume from the Yorks, and even a box of stationery from Mr. Gardner, who had insisted on bringing something once he heard it was Paige's birthday.

It wasn't until they were through eating ham and potato salad, baked beans and buns, cake and ice cream, that Paige realized there had been no gift from Bryan.

The last bites of birthday cake went down with some difficulty. It's hard to swallow and choke back tears, Paige discovered.

It was quiet on the porch.

Mrs. Smead had gone inside to lie down.

Mike, Mr. York, and Mr. Gardner were discussing the relative merits of their favorite baseball teams.

Mrs. York, Lois, and Ellen had disappeared with the dirty dishes.

Most amazing of all, Beth and Evan had taken Bonzo and Blackie to the far corner of the yard to play fetch.

Paige and Bryan were left alone.

"Paige?"

"Hmmm?" She didn't want to appear hurt because he hadn't given her a present. After all, the York family had given her one. And she was no baby.

"Want to take a walk?"

"Why not?" She sounded more casual than she felt.

They sauntered over to Lady Blue in the pasture. The little horse pranced merrily to greet them and nudged Paige's pockets for sugar.

"I'm sorry I didn't give you a gift up there on the porch." Bryan's voice was soft.

"That's okay."

"I wanted to save it till we were alone."

She turned to stare at him. Suddenly the tears were close, but for a different reason. "You did?"

"Uh-huh." He pulled a tiny box from his shirt pocket. It was wrapped in foil paper and a tiny piece of silver ribbon, the kind Carlson's Jewelers used. "Here."

Paige noticed that her hands were shaking when she reached to take it. She flicked her fingernail along the inside of the wrap. It fell away. A velvet box. Nervously, she opened it.

Inside lay a delicate gold chain. Suspended from the chain were two gold numbers, a one and a six, welded side by side. Sixteen.

"Ohhh," she gasped. "It's beautiful!"

"Do you like it? Really?" For the first time she could remember, Bryan seemed unsure.

"Like it? I *love* it!"

"Good." He expelled the word with a gusty sigh. "I don't buy very many presents for girls. I wasn't sure I'd get the right thing."

Paige bit her lip to prevent herself from telling him that *anything* he might have chosen would have pleased her.

"I'm going to put it on right away," she told him, lifting the chain from its box with trembling fingers.

"Here, let me help you," he offered as she struggled with the tiny clasp.

When he was done, he turned her by the shoulders. "There. How's that?"

She ran an exploratory finger across the necklace. It skimmed her collarbone. "A perfect fit."

"Sweet sixteen," he said, smiling.

Paige nodded. Indeed it was sweet to be sixteen. A lot of wonderful things had already happened. God had truly blessed her family. She had a new uncle; a nice, kind, generous man. And she felt she had a new cousin as well. The old Evan had been lost in the torrent of love and understanding he'd been experiencing these past days. The new Evan was more secure, more relaxed, more fun.

She'd solved a mystery! A real one—just like the fictional detectives she admired.

Even Mrs. Smead had been taken care of, thanks to Samuel Gardner. Because of Sarah's son, she did not have to live out her days in poverty. And, of course, she had Beth and Bryan. They were becoming more dear to her every day.

Nightfall was coming. The smells and sounds of a summer evening lingered in the air. The sun was dipping lower in the west, making a final blaze before it settled into twilight.

Lady Blue nudged her hip. Paige moved away from the curious nose and toward Bryan.

"Do you remember what the last part of that saying is?" His voice startled her.

"What?"

"Sweet sixteen. Do remember the rest?"

"Of course, sweet sixteen and never been kissed . . ." Her voice trailed away. Suddenly she was embarrassed.

"Is that you?" Bryan's voice held a note of laughter. Paige knew he could see the blush on her cheeks.

"Sixteen? I've been sixteen all day long," she parried.

"How about the last part?"

Paige sighed. "You should know that. My dad said I couldn't even *date* till I was sixteen. How could I . . ." She stopped. Bryan was smiling at her with a certain look, both tender and teasing, in his eyes.

"I can't do anything about the dating part right now," he murmured. "I'll try to fix that next weekend. And well, about the other . . ." His eyes hinted at more than words now could.

Paige wasn't sure if it was the last flashes of the evening sun or fireworks or some strange phenomenon inside her brain, but suddenly her world was bright with stars.

No matter how many summers I have, Paige mused, *there will never be another quite like this one.*

With Bryan's arm over her shoulders, they walked back across the pasture.